things i shouldn't think

ALSO BY JANET RUTH YOUNG

The Opposite of Music

My Beautiful Failure

things i shouldn't think

janet ruth young

atheneum
Atheneum Books for Young Readers
New York London Toronto Sydney New Delhi

ATHENEUM BOOKS FOR YOUNG READERS
An imprint of Simon & Schuster Children's Publishing Division
1230 Avenue of the Americas, New York, New York 10020

This book is a work of fiction. Any references to historical events, real people, or real locales are used fictitiously. Other names, characters, places, and incidents are products of the author's imagination, and any resemblance to actual events or locales or persons, living or dead, is entirely coincidental.

First Atheneum Books for Young Readers paperback edition November 2012

Also available in an Atheneum Books for Young Readers hardcover edition.
Previously published as *The Babysitter Murders*
For information about special discounts for bulk purchases, please contact Simon & Schuster Special Sales at 1-866-506-1949 or business@simonandschuster.com.
The Simon & Schuster Speakers Bureau can bring authors to your live event.
For more information or to book an event, contact the Simon & Schuster Speakers Bureau at 1-866-248-3049 or visit our website at www.simonspeakers.com.
Book design by Debra Sfetsios-Conover
The text of this book is set in Weiss Std.
2 4 6 8 10 9 7 5 3 1
CIP data for this book is available from the Library of Congress.
ISBN 978-1-4169-5944-1 (hardcover)
ISBN 978-1-4424-5107-0 (paperback)
ISBN 978-1-4424-5925-0 (eBook)

FOR TONY HILLIARD, AND FOR ALL THE DANI SOLOMONS

ACKNOWLEDGMENTS

Thanks to the people who contributed to this book by answering questions and allowing me to interview or observe them: Shep Abbott, David Allen, Liz Duff, and Alexander Thompson; Tony Hilliard, formerly of the Rockport Police Department, and his son, Nick Hilliard; Ray Lamont of the *Gloucester Times*; and Amanda Roeder and the Marblehead High School Jewel Tones. Appreciation to my writing group—Cassandra Oxley and Jan Voogd—and my sister Diane Young, for being supportive critical readers. Much gratitude to Kimberly A. Glazier of the Ferkauf Graduate School of Psychology, Yeshiva University, for lending her expertise and for reviewing several drafts. And warmest thanks to my editor, Gretchen Hirsch, who loved, understood, and helped to develop this story.

part 1 THE LINE

1

MyFace Profile

Name: Dani

Sex: Female

Age: 17 years old

Location: Hawthorne, Massachusetts, United States

Last log-in: April 23

Mood: romantic

My hobbies: tennis, running, singing

Interested in: friendship male and female, dating male, relationship male

My favorite quote:

"Watch your thoughts, for they become words. Watch your words, for they become actions. Watch your actions, for they become habits. Watch your habits, for they become character. Watch your character, for it becomes your destiny."—Charles Reade

About me:

Hello, world!!! I'm a jr. at Hawthorne High and sing alto in our a cappella group the Hawtones . . . love the teamwork . . . play varsity tennis . . . brings out my competitive side . . . best friend is Shelley . . . u can see lots of pictures of us here . . . lots of good times . . . I'm a loyal friend, always try to live up to what is expected of me . . . hate letting people down, would rather be disappointed in them than have them disappointed in me . . . I've had this happen to me at least once since my dad moved away when I was little . . . I won't bore you with that story since you probably know how that goes . . . I like a guy at school, but he has no idea . . . so if you are cute and reasonably tall and above all, NICE, please hit me up.

TMI, Dani thinks. *That's way too much information. Just leave in the happy parts.*

Hello, world!!! I'm a jr. at Hawthorne High and sing alto in our a cappella group the Hawtones . . . love the teamwork . . . play varsity tennis . . . brings out my competitive side . . . best friend is Shelley . . . u can see lots of pictures of us here . . . lots of good times . . . I'm a loyal friend, always try to live up to what is expected of me . . . if you are cute and reasonably tall and above all, NICE, please hit me up.

Dani presses Publish.

2

Dani Solomon babysits for a boy named Alex Draper three times a week. Dani doesn't like having so many nights tied up. She doesn't need the money, either. Her mother is a successful real estate broker and gives Dani a big allowance. But Dani keeps babysitting because Alex and his mom—whose name is Cynthia Draper but whom Alex calls "Mrs. Alex," so Dani calls her that too—rely on her. Dani's sure she's the most responsible, educational, and fun babysitter Mrs. Alex could find. Plus, she likes Alex because he makes her laugh.

On April 23, Alex and Dani play Lion King, a game Alex made up after watching the movie.

"You're not a mountain anymore," Alex says. "You're fire."

"I thought we were both mountains," says Dani. It's hard to keep track of all the characters, scenes, and events that weren't in the movie.

"I'm still a mountain. But you're fire. So flame up."

Dani hisses and waves her fingers. "Am I flaming up?"

Alex stands his plastic animals at their paper-cup caves. They rear up and sniff the flames.

"So what does a mountain do?"

"Watch." Alex squats and grunts like he's trying to poop. "See? Now I'm a mountain. Do that when you turn back."

"A grisly discovery in Dorchester this afternoon," says the living room TV. "A nine-year-old girl allegedly stabbed to death by her stepfather. Details at six." Dani grabs the remote to shut off the set. She sees a three-decker apartment building cordoned by yellow tape. A small lump covered by a blanket lies in the middle of a big stretcher. Two sobbing neighbors watch a man leave in handcuffs.

Monster, she thinks. Or is he just crazy? What kind of person would do that? And how could he do that to a little kid? The girl probably trusted her stepfather the way Alex trusts Dani. Dani imagines something like that happening to Alex. Alex as a lump on a stretcher. Alex having been killed by someone he trusted. Someone close to him, who is supposed to be responsible for him. A caregiver, just like Dani. The idea is too horrible.

Alex's animals form a circle on the coffee table, waiting for the lion to tell them what to do. Dani pauses while the scene in her mind completes itself in greater detail. She imagines being a murderer like the man in Dorchester. She pictures herself walking in handcuffs to a police cruiser in front of Alex's house. Mrs. Alex watches with an accusing, tear-stained face. Or worse, an ambulance pulls up to the emergency room where Mrs. Alex works, and Mrs. Alex realizes that the lump on the stretcher is her own child. Ugh. *Oh my God, it's too awful,* Dani thinks. She shivers and puts her hands over her face. *Stop thinking about this,* Dani tells herself. *Now.*

That's my TMI, Dani thinks. *Too much imagination.* She finds it easy to imagine herself into all kinds of situations. Her imagination helps with writing assignments and with making up games for Alex, but it also gives her trouble. During rehearsal for her a cappella group she often pictures herself on vacation in Aruba with Gordon Abt, and she can almost feel her beach dress clinging to her legs as she and Gordy run hand in hand through the waves. Sometimes she worries that the other Hawtones can read her expression: unfocused eyes, parted lips, a small gasp escaping from her mouth because she forgot where she was and thought that the vacation was really happening . . .

Now her TMI is making her imagine being like someone she would never empathize with in a million years. Dani is not a violent person. She detests people who are hurtful or violent. She tries very hard not to hurt others, not even their feelings. No way in the world would she ever even strike a child. Dani decides to boycott all violent movies and TV shows. Maybe the stuff she sees—even glimpses accidentally—is putting pictures in her head. Maybe what her health teacher said was true: Violent stuff changes the way your mind works.

"Now be a mountain so the lion can stand on you and look far," says Alex.

"Is this far enough?" Dani asks Alex. She squats, grunts like she's going to poop, then lifts Alex and his lion up to the ceiling. Alex loves that, and Mrs. Alex is too short to do it. Now Dani thinks only about Alex. She forgets about the Dorchester girl and her stepfather.

3

Gordon Abt is massaging Dani's shoulders. This is real life, not Dani's imagination. Before every rehearsal, the Hawtones massage the singer on their left and then the singer on their right. Dani stands beside Gordy because she's an alto and he's a tenor.

He touches her lightly, but Dani feels her nerves tingle all the way to the floor.

"Ahh," she says. She says it ironically, so that if he doesn't share her feelings she can pretend to be joking. But Shelley hears her. Shelley knows that Dani's being ironic about being ironic; that she really does mean *Ahh*.

Dani's tall, but Gordy is taller. Although only his hands touch Dani, she senses his whole body. It shimmers in parallel to hers like a six-foot sheet of glass filled with afternoon sun.

Now it's her turn to massage him. His shoulders are slender but have some muscle. As Dani massages, her heart pounds a word—*look, look*—and she feels like their pairing stands out from all the others.

When she lets go of his shimmer, he thanks her the way he would thank anybody for anything. The Hawtones begin their vocal exercises, starting at a low pitch and rising by half-steps.

Nathan Brandifield, a baritone, smiles at Dani every time she sings a note. He's geeky and she doesn't know him well, but he's always oddly proud of her.

"New music for June fourth," their music director, Mr. Gabler, says. "Well, not new to the seniors, but the rest of you need to learn it. This time anyone—male or female—can audition to sing lead, and we'll all decide who sounds best."

What is the song, and who will be the soloist? Last week Dani suggested "Fix You" by Coldplay because she thought it would be perfect for Gordon's voice. She even bought the sheet music for Mr. Gabler, hoping to tip the scales. Gordy suggested "Back on the Chain Gang" by the Pretenders, which, coincidentally, Dani loves and sings well. Shelley asked Meghan Dimmock, a soprano, what she wanted to sing, as if the new song was already Meghan's. Shelley is a good singer too. Why didn't Shelley suggest something that showcases her own talents?

"Retread," a senior mutters as she hands around the music. The new/old song is Mr. Gabler's arrangement of "Old Cape Cod," originally recorded by Patti Page. The Hawtones would prefer a mix of new and classic music, but Mr. Gabler has a weakness for all songs pertaining to Massachusetts. He plays last year's concert recording on his computer.

Nathan is a sophomore prodigy. He memorizes most songs by the second rehearsal, and he can imitate the sounds of twenty-five instruments. He listens by tilting his head, as if his ear were a bowl the music was being poured into.

When the song ends, Meghan adjusts her top to show more midriff. Meghan's a junior, and everyone says she'll get a music scholarship. Dani doesn't care for her singing, but Meghan has a knack for attracting attention and striking photogenic poses that might sell tickets. Gabler favors her too. He usually doesn't stop the song when she goes off key.

"Places," Gabler says. "Let's run it through once."

The group makes a tight semicircle that lets the singers see every performer and hear every voice. The vibrations from their throats meet in the center, making a thick column of sound. Dani loves feeling her voice knock on the door of other voices and find them completely solid.

"You're the best suited to 'Cape Cod,'" Nathan tells Dani during a break. "You sound the most like Patti Page."

At home by herself, Dani is a great singer, but she's afraid to sing lead with the Hawtones. If they do a love song and she looks at Gordy, she might choke. And in a cappella music no instruments cover your errors, so every flaw is magnified. The Hawtones' semicircle is one being, one organism, a giant C of closeness. In performance the singers cue one another with a tiny look, a foot shift, the lift of a shoulder. *My turn. Your turn. Sing louder. I need to clear my throat; can you fill in?* Except for Meghan's pitch problems, the Hawtones never miss a note or a lyric. If Dani sang lead and faltered, she'd hurt the whole group.

Dani still squirms over a mistake she made last fall. Shelley was out with a cold, and Mr. Gabler gave Dani two copies of a new song they had to learn quickly. Dani meant to deliver one copy to Shelley's house, but she was thinking about Gordy all the way home, and even when she played tennis with Shelley that weekend she didn't think to mention the song.

The following Monday Gabler said, "Get out 'Charlie on the MTA'" and Shelley said, "We have a new song?" Mr. Gabler said, "Didn't you give Shelley her music?" And they both looked at Dani like she had seventeen-year-old Alzheimer's and Dani wished she could drop through the floor into the boiler room where no one went except the janitor, and way down to the core of the earth, banging on every surface and object along the way. Mr. Gabler called Dani's mistake "a failure to execute."

Dani wasn't stupid, and she couldn't blame it on Alzheimer's. She inventoried her motives. *Do I hate Shelley? Do I see Shelley as a rival? Did I set her up? Do I want Shelley to fail?* She later apologized to Shelley for "the Charlie incident" until Shelley asked her to shut up. Now Dani wonders again, *Am I a crappy friend?*

Dani needs to forget the incident, so she focuses on Mr. Gabler. His thinning hair; his L.L. Bean polo shirt in an unflattering shade of electric blue; his tan pants that have been through the dryer so many times that when he turns his back he has a case of VPL (visible panty line), which is especially unfortunate in a man. Apparently Gabler wears briefs, not boxers. This is TMVI. Too much visual information.

Mr. Gabler signals the altos to sing louder. "Give me more," he says. He winks at Dani. He must have forgiven her for the sheet music. *Why am I still thinking about the Charlie incident?* she wonders. Everyone else has moved on.

Dani begins to relax, but then, without wanting to, she pictures herself reaching out and cupping Mr. Gabler's testicles. *Oh my God,* she thinks. *That's so disgusting.* If she were alone, Dani would shudder and put her hands over her face. Although she's been staring at Mr. Gabler's thin pants and VPL, the idea of grabbing his genitals has come out of nowhere. *No, no, no,* Dani thinks. *Make this thought go away!*

But instead, more details flood into her mind. How his briefs are probably worn thin too. That's two icky layers of thin material. How his scrotum would feel making contact with her hand. Revolting. And the worst thing: Mr. Gabler's reaction. How shocked he would be. How shocked that she would do something like that, when he thought she was a worthwhile and valuable member of the group. Her image of his expression is so detailed that it seems real. Dani has to look at her hands to make sure they're not touching Mr. Gabler.

But he's okay. Nothing has happened.

"Dani," Gabler says in his usual way. "You with us?"

Dani nods and sings louder. Her left palm tingles as if it's had contact with Gabler's privates. When Gabler turns to the baritones, Dani rubs her hands together. *It seemed so real. Did I really touch him?* she wonders. But no one looks shocked. No one yells or stares or reacts. While Dani tries to focus on the music, her imagination keeps running ahead. Now it fills in all the reactions of her group mates. Meghan, Shelley, Gordon—what would they think? *I guess she's not getting that solo. I guess she's not my friend anymore. Well, she's kinda cute, but I guess she's plain crazy.*

Dani closes her eyes for a minute. She feels panicky. Maybe she'll have to drop out of Hawtones. She doesn't know how she can keep coming to practice if Mr. Gabler's VPL continues to show.

She brushes her left hand against her skirt.

"Hey, Shell," Dani asks after class, "did I seem . . . weird in there? Was I acting unusual?"

"Weird and unusual how?"

"Well . . ." *What can I say?* "Did I seem to interact, like, oddly with Mr. Gabler? Or did I move differently?"

"You closed your eyes when Gordy was massaging you. You turned red a few times. So no, nothing unusual for you. If you didn't turn into a goofball around Gordy, that would be unusual."

"My knees felt rubbery right then," Dani says. "I could hardly stand up."

"Will you try for that lead?" Shelley asks.

"Not if Meghan wants it."

"What Meghan wants," Shelley responds, "Meghan gets. And that's the way it should be." She sticks "Old Cape Cod" into her backpack as they head to lunch.

4

Kinda cute. That was how Malcolm Pinto would describe Dani and her pal. Dani is a little too tall, a little too athletic, a little too everything, and that a cappella crowd is too smiley and sunshiney, as if an enema of Tang, Gummi Bear vitamins, and major chords has been shoved up their butts.

But getting back to Dani. She has a long, tall tennis build—square shoulders from walloping those serves, no hips, and in between a stretched-out triangle. The only thing that saves Dani from seeming like a rich bitch is that everything touching her seems like it's been hung in the sun on a really bright day. Her clothes look brighter and whiter than anyone else's, like the outfit she has on now, a pink hoodie over a white ribbed tank top and a faded denim skirt. The bits of jewelry she wears are made of string or rope, as if she made them from scraps on the deck of a sailboat. Her hair is reddish blond (Malcolm's dad, who likes to help Malcolm evaluate the looks of the various high school girls, corrected him once by saying "strawberry blond," savoring the term as if he was reading something nice off a menu) with pale gold glimmers that are probably natural. She's hot, but her hotness is combined with another term. He hates to say it: She's *merry*.

Shelley is cute too, in a smaller, darker way. She has the sparkpluggy, power-at-the-core type of tennis build, and she wears simple clothes like polo shirts and bandannas and high-top sneakers. "That's a baby dyke if I've ever seen one," Malcolm's dad, Michael Pinto, said when Malcolm pointed her out. Malcolm had felt admiration for his dad, who, because of his police work, not only knew what went on in the world, but had a shorthand term for any situation you could come across. "Nothing new under the sun, my boy," he would say. "Nothing your old man hasn't seen before."

Malcolm takes a drag off his cigarette and watches the two girls come into the courtyard.

5

"Let's eat outside," Shelley says. "I need to talk."

It's not a great day. Drizzle sticks to the air like a coating of hairspray. But Dani and Shelley don't mind because they're outdoor fiends, the sporty type. Other outdoor fiends, nicotine addicts like Malcolm Pinto, stand behind the potted shrubs near Dani's favorite bench, hiding cigarettes under their sleeves. Others are nature lovers who relate better to trees, clouds, and grass than to people. Still others are antisocial, and the courtyard is the farthest from their peers they can get.

"What's up?" Dani asks when they open their dips. Since they met in day care, they've called lunch "dips." Each of them brings a dip and dipper to share: Cheez-Its with yogurt, cashews with mango salsa, Oreos with peanut butter.

"I need to tell you something," Shelley says. She looks scared, serious. *Will today be the day?* Dani wonders.

Shelley tucks her bangs inside her hat. "You and I have spent a lot of years together."

"True," Dani says.

"And we agree on a lot of things."

Dani nods.

"We've got a ton of stuff in common."

"Uh-huh."

"We have a lot of the same opinions? We view life the same way?" A question has crept into Shelley's voice, making Dani nod again.

"But there's a difference between us. And it's as big as it can be between best friends."

"What do you mean?" Dani asks.

"I'm gay, Dani." Shelley takes a deep breath. "I'm gay. That's what I need to tell you."

What can Dani say? She can say "I know." But that would spoil Shelley's dramatic moment. Still, Dani does know. And she's waited years for Shelley to tell her what she already knows.

When they were ten or eleven, Shelley would claim to like the boy most other girls liked, as if crushes were decided by acclamation and not by a sickening, weakening, all-consuming feeling in your gut that said *This one and no other*. Shelley would pass notes saying "OMG he is adorable," but the notes rang false. Since junior high, Shelley's been quick to defend various airheaded girls Dani dislikes, girls who act narcissistic, which Shelley interprets as confidence. Those two things set Shelley apart from most other girls Dani knew. Once, during a high school tennis match, a spectator told the person next to her, "That girl's a lesbo. Look at the way she walks." Dani went to the sidelines and said, "All of us jock girls walk like that," and the woman kept her mouth shut for the rest of the match.

And last winter, Dani and Shelley were shopping in a music store downtown when two women walked in. They had short haircuts and wore similar black parkas, and although they were white, one pushed an Asian toddler in a stroller.

"Look at those two," a college-aged guy in the guitar section said. "Look at the twins. Hey, are you two sisters?"

"My mommy is a resbian," his friend said in a fake Chinese accent, and the guys around him snickered. Shelley laughed too, but she looked as if her own life sucked and the women's lives sucked and she couldn't imagine life ever not sucking.

"Jerks!" Dani yelled at the guys. "Jerks, jerks, jerks!" She grabbed Shelley's sleeve and pulled her around the block where they could have their pictures taken with a giant elf and get free hot chocolate. Then she started waiting, thinking, *Any day now she'll tell me.*

Still, today she can't decide how to react to an announcement that was intended to surprise Dani and make their friendship closer. If she acts surprised, she'll be dishonest to her best friend. If she says "I know," she'll mock Shelley's courage and make Shelley look ridiculous.

"Dani," Shelley repeats. "Did you hear me? I just came out to you. I'm gay."

Dani notices, over Shelley's shoulder, Malcolm Pinto watching them. Can he hear what Shelley's saying?

"You're shocked," Shelley says. "You don't know what to say."

"No."

"You're the first one I'm coming out to, you know."

Dani fiddles with a pack of cookies. "How long have you known?"

"A couple of years. Don't tell anyone, Dani."

"What about the Gay-Straight Alliance?" Dani asks. "Are you

out there?" Theoretically, gay students at Hawthorne High have a lot of support. At least sixty kids are part of the GSA—they overflowed the classroom the day it was formed. Three gay teachers advise the club.

"You don't think people in the GSA are necessarily that supportive, do you?" Shelley says. "That's just the hot organization to belong to. It looks really open-minded but in fact it's a load of crap."

"Wow," Dani says. "I assumed everyone in the club was sincere."

"Don't kid yourself." Shelley closes her tub of pepperoni with mustard. "It's still as hard as ever to be gay. Or lesbian, or not sure what you are."

"You know better than I do whether people in the club are prejudiced," Dani shrugs. "Maybe people in school act different around me. More accepting."

"That's because you're straight."

"But they thought you were straight, didn't they?"

Shelley stares like Dani is obtuse. Dani watches the kids sneaking smokes behind Shelley. Malcolm is dramatically furtive. He smokes Camels without filters and usually goes back inside sporting tobacco in his teeth.

"I'm not shocked," Dani finally says. "You are my best friend and I love you no matter what." Immediately she regrets the "no matter what," because it suggests there's something wrong with being gay. The right words and the wrong words are tying Dani up in knots. Again she wishes she could tell Shelley she had already known.

Shelley wraps an arm around Dani, and they tilt their heads together as they have since day care. "I love you too, no matter what," Shelley says. But it feels awkward.

Dani waits for Shelley to tell her more. To talk about some bad times. Being embarrassed. Being rejected and feeling left out. Overhearing that joke in the music store and not knowing how to react. Or maybe Shelley wants to talk a new way, an open way, about the person she likes. Dani would overlook Shelley's weakness for narcissistic people.

"So, are you . . . involved with anyone?" Dani asks. "Or do you want to be?"

"I haven't gotten involved with anyone yet," Shelley says. She touches the bangs falling from her hat. "Dani, this has to be a secret. It has to be, because of my parents. It wouldn't be okay with them."

Dani pictures Shelley as a vulnerable creature being born. Just cracking from an egg, her skin a delicate membrane more easily bruised than Dani's. The shell of the egg is lavender, the color of the Gay-Straight Alliance. Shelley may seem tough, but people must treat her delicately. Dani holds the eggshell of Shelley's gayness in her hand. *How does she know I won't crush it?* She imagines saying something hideous to Shelley, that she doesn't fit in, that she is evil. *You are a freak,* she pictures herself saying. *You are unfit to be my friend. Or my tennis partner.*

No! No! Dani thinks. *Shelley is not a freak. She is a great friend and an awesome person. I would never intentionally say something so hurtful to Shelley.* Still, she feels nervous, like the wrong word will leap out.

A person could say anything, right? A person could be a great friend one day and then lose control and become a sucky, mean friend the next. The courtyard seems to brim with nasty possibilities.

Dani sits up straight and looks into Shelley's eyes. "You are my best friend," she says. "I will absolutely keep your secret."

"Thanks," Shelley says. She holds on to the rubber tips of her sneakers, and she looks like the little kid Dani met in day care. "I feel better knowing that someone knows."

"It's an honor to be the first." There. That's something true. "Can you hit for a while right at two fifteen?" Dani asks. "I feel like some of the shots I used to be sure of have gotten inconsistent."

Shelley sits back as if she's been struck by something. "I can't believe I just poured my guts out to you and you're already talking about tennis. I still have a weird out-of-body feeling from coming out to you." She wipes the front of her cargo pants as if her embarrassment is a bunch of cracker crumbs that a dab of peanut butter is causing to stick.

Oh no, Dani thinks. *I can't do anything right.*

6

Later that afternoon, Dani jumps up the steps to Alex's. She's running late. She felt bad about Shelley getting short shrift at lunch, so she mentioned Shelley's orientation again after their tennis practice. They flopped onto the grass, and the conversation about being gay turned into a conversation about Meghan that used up Dani's travel time.

Alex appears inside the screen door.

"Sorry, guy," Dani says.

"Mom's mad, but not a lot mad."

As she enters he backs up, talking the whole time. "Do you want to see my new e-Pet? It's a horse named Louie."

"Sorry!" Dani yells upstairs.

"It's okay!" Mrs. Alex yells back. From the sound of things, Mrs. Alex is talking to the hospital, putting on her heels, and styling her hair all at once. "Glad to know you made it, that's all."

Of course I made it. When have I ever not made it? Dani thinks.

Dani hates letting people down, especially Alex and Mrs. Alex. Alex is so cute and heartbreaking. Alex's father left when Alex was only four. Dani tries to be extra fun so Alex won't miss his dad. She should have told Shelley she was pressed for time, but that would have meant letting Shelley down. Whenever Dani gets too busy, someone in her life gets cheated, and today it's Alex.

But there will be compensation. Because he sometimes asks about her matches, Dani used some of her babysitting money to buy him a junior racket, a really good one with the same features as hers but only twenty-one inches long. She wants to give him lessons once a week when school's out. Maybe when Alex gets to Hawthorne High he'll be captain of the boys' team.

"I'll go calm your mother down," she tells Alex.

"There you are!" Mrs. Alex says. She wears a lab coat but snazzes things up with silver hoop earrings and pink lipstick.

"Anything new with the kiddo?" Dani asks.

Mrs. Alex is a nurse practitioner, which she says is as good as a doctor. She's distracted most of the time, but in many ways she's easier to talk to than Dani's mom. She has a philosophy that Dani can get behind. She's been through some rough times, but she believes that no matter what, you have to place a high value on yourself. She was in love with Alex's father at the beginning, and tells exciting stories about meeting him on a sailboat and him getting five passengers through a thunderstorm. She thought he owned the sailboat, but friends told her later he didn't. Then followed a year-by-year landslide of her admiration, and eventually she realized that he was not good enough for her, and she asked him to leave. Now she only mentions him when she has to, not using his name (Patrick) or the phrase "my ex-husband" but the phrase "Alex's father." That makes it seem like Patrick is someone in Alex's life but not Mrs. Alex's—a friend of Alex whom Alex had once introduced her to. Alex talks about Patrick when his mom isn't around. He tells stories about feats of heroism, like flying a helicopter through the middle of an iceberg. Maybe all those adventures spring from the sailboat story, and Alex carries in his genes the infatuation Mrs. Alex first felt when meeting Patrick. Dani thinks of Alex's version as Tarzan Daddy.

What can she do with Alex for the next eight hours to compensate for his losing his adventurous father? And will there be anything for her to eat when she gives Alex his supper? Mrs. Alex keeps promising she'll stock up on food for Dani, but she usually forgets. Often there's been nothing for Alex, either, and Dani walks him the six blocks to McDonald's.

Mrs. Alex jingles her keys. "Nothing really new. He still has a slight ear infection. I'll be home after eleven."

How does that feel, bitch?

Dani has a picture of herself getting the junior racket from Alex's room and whacking the side of Mrs. Alex's head. Mrs. Alex's eyes roll up. She sways for a minute before hitting the ground. *Not Mrs. Alex. Not Mrs. Alex. I would never hit or hurt her. I would complain about her, sure, but I would never hit or hurt her. I wouldn't call her the* B *word either. I basically like Mrs. Alex. I don't know why I would even think that.* While having all these thoughts, Dani listens to Mrs. Alex talk. She tries to focus on her employer's instructions. She touches her own lips to make sure she hasn't spoken while Mrs. Alex is speaking. That she hasn't said the *B* word. The vision of Mrs. Alex collapsing was so real that Dani goes to Alex's room to check that the racket is still where she left it. She touches her mouth again and rubs her hands. Then she follows Mrs. Alex downstairs.

When Dani sees the TV she remembers that murder in Dorchester. She had forgotten about it since Saturday. She remembers that she thought about Alex being murdered. She pictured him on a stretcher, under a blanket. It was awful. It was upsetting. It wasn't real and it didn't happen. She made herself stop thinking about it. Then they played some more and she felt better. They ate chicken and she did her homework. After she put him to bed she checked him once an hour and he was fine. But now the pictures come back, although she tries to push them aside. She doesn't understand why they're back again, since she thought she dealt with them last time. Now Dani imagines Alex lying on his bedroom floor with a kitchen knife beside his body. All the stuff that's usually inside is showing. She talks extra loud to drive the thought away.

"Have a good night at work!" she tells Mrs. Alex, putting her hand on Alex's shoulder.

This is bad, Dani thinks. *I feel terrible and I just got here. What's wrong with me?*

Mrs. Alex stops in the doorway. "What about you? How was school? How's *the boy?*"

"He has no idea. It's painful. You know."

"Louie's a boy," Alex says. "Do you want to see him?"

Dani has tons of homework, but she pities Alex for the usual reasons, so she sits with him at the computer. She puts her arm around Alex but she feels funny touching him, because even though she hasn't said or done anything wrong, she's ashamed. She's ashamed of her imagination and her thoughts. She wants more than anything to relax and stop working her mind so hard and be normal. Mrs. Alex will be gone for eight hours tonight. *Will I be having these thoughts the whole time I'm here?* Dani wonders.

7

Dani and Shelley warm up for their match with Monsignor Deagle High School.

"Oh my God, is she cute," Shelley says when they collect the balls.

"She is cute," Dani agrees. Since the coming-out, the word *she* with no antecedent always means Meghan Dimmock. Dani is giving Shelley a free pass on talking about Meghan. A lifetime of crushes has backed up inside her, after all. It will take weeks of talking before she catches up with the straight people.

Dani hopes more of her fellow Schooners arrive early so she and Shelley can practice on the same side of the net. Lately she's been missing a lot of shots that come down the center line. Their coach hinted at making Dani and Shelley co-captains next year, but that chance could evaporate. Wouldn't it be weird if Shelley was captain by herself? Or worse, if she co-captained with another player? Dani would be jealous.

"You don't think she's dumb, do you?" Shelley asks. "Because I can't honestly like a dumb person. I can think they're hot, sure, but they can't be my first real girlfriend. I can only admire them from a distance."

"I don't know, Shell. Are you reading her correctly? Is it that she's dumb? Or does she just not pay attention to other people?"

"That's because she's concentrating. She's so into her music that she blocks everything else out."

"Maybe. And, you know, there are different forms of intelligence. Musical intelligence, for one." Dani never lies outright, so she doesn't say Meghan has musical intelligence, only that it is a form.

"Have you heard of kinesthetic intelligence?" Shelley asks. "It's like coordination. It's the intelligence that makes you not hit into the net just because Gordon Abt walked by."

"I'm not looking at him." She isn't. But every day she remembers what color shirt he's wearing so her eyes can scan for that color. And sometimes she likes thinking about him without talking about him. Not talking makes her feelings compress and intensify, like the grain of sand that forms a pearl in an oyster, or the piece of coal that gets pressed into a diamond, and every precious and semiprecious cliché ever written. She sees a plum-colored shirt hesitate by the fence, but she stares down the center line at Shelley until the color moves on. He'll probably admire her dedication to improving her game.

Another reason not to talk about Gordy is to spare him the insult of being parallel to Meghan. Gordon is super competent. In addition to singing in the Hawtones he plays French horn in the band. He's been captain of the All-State band and even played on the lawn of the White House. He hasn't told a lot of people, but Malia Obama smiled at him. Malia has a great smile, Gordon said. When Dani heard that, it was like a knife going through her; that was how she first knew she liked him.

"I think her favorite fruit is raspberries," Shelley is saying.

Dani watches the Deagle bus pull up and their coach greet the Hawthorne coach. Malcolm Pinto slouches on the handball court, hiding his cigarette, watching the girls hop off the bus. The Deagle captain, Zoe Brightman, already has a great tan, and her legs glow with lotion. Dani knows which girls are attractive, but it's hard to imagine liking girls more than boys.

Look, here's the lesbo! I'm playing tennis with a lesbo! These words ring in Dani's head, a nasty taunt in a nasty voice like the one in the music store. *No!* Dani protests inside. *No!* Trying to push the words away before she says them. *That's awful. That's cruel. That's disgusting.* She has never thought anything so wrong.

What is this? Am I going crazy? How hideous it would be if Dani outed Shelley—not just by whispering her secret to one Hawthorne kid, but by shouting the crudest thing she could think of before a major tennis match in front of her teammates, the Deagle varsity and junior varsity teams, both coaches, Malcolm Pinto and some of his nic-addicted friends, five members of the student council leaving a meeting, and three parents walking to their cars? The fear that she's going to yell "Lesbo!" builds inside her. Dani has searched her soul and is pretty sure she's not homophobic, but would that stop her from yelling something? Why has Shelley placed this lavender egg in Dani's hand? Shelley winds up for her serve, shaking the bangs out of her eyes. Has Dani yelled "Lesbo"? She touches her mouth to make sure her lips aren't moving. Then she focuses on the ball's *thwop*, as regular as a metronome. She touches her mouth a few more times, but by mid-match, thank God, she's forgotten about outing Shelley.

8

A Deagle player leaps in the air to deflect a ball that would have dropped behind her. Malcolm shares the joy she must feel. Inwardly he knows he's athletic, even though he's never developed that facet of himself. *I know what they think of me,* he acknowledges, while the players switch sides on the court. *I know I seem like a skinny fringey guy who doesn't have much going on. But when I enroll in the academy they'll see who I really am.*

Malcolm's dad, uncle, and grandfather have all been cops. Like boot camp, the police academy takes raw material and molds it into steel. But although he knows he can handle the physical part of training, his true talent lies in the psychological and forensic side of the job. He will become a detective and bust up narcotics networks, fencing schemes, and child-pornography rings.

His dad, Michael, was lucky to work on some cases that went beyond the normal run of small-town crime. Some drug dealers from Boston once rented a beachfront motel and attempted to whet the local appetite for crack cocaine. They brought a sixteen-year-old girl, the relative of one of the dealers if you can believe it, to offer as a prostitute. While the feds went after the drug evidence, Michael carried the girl out in her shortie nightgown.

That night the bust appeared on all the Boston TV stations. Michael and Malcolm watched while Mrs. Pinto sat beside her husband on the arm of the couch. The perps, in handcuffs, had pulled their shirts and jackets over their faces so they couldn't be seen. Naïve summer tourists witnessed this walk of shame.

Michael pointed to the astonished tourists and the blurred-out face of the girl.

"You see them?" he said. "Those innocent people? They're like sheep."

He pointed to the perps in handcuffs. "They're the wolves who go after the sheep."

He turned to Malcolm. "People like you and me, we're the sheepdogs. We keep the wolves away from the sheep."

9

Dani studies "Old Cape Cod." Her mind fast-forwards to the concert, where she sings the lead perfectly while smiling a better smile than Malia Obama's. During the final bow Gordy sneaks backstage. He returns with an armload of flowers for Dani. Everyone cheers.

Dani's mom, Beth Solomon, knocks on the bedroom door. Beth has short hair the same color as Dani's, nearly invisible red eyelashes that she defines with three coats of black mascara, and freckles she hides with foundation.

"How's Alex?" she asks.

"He has an ear infection. And he's poignant."

"Who would he have if he didn't have you?"

"His mom?"

"His mom. Well."

Beth used to feel sorry for Mrs. Alex, but she lost sympathy when Mrs. Alex lied to Dani. Mrs. Alex claimed to be working extra hours at the hospital but instead went dancing with one of the EMTs at a bar outside town. "Might as well make a night of it," Mrs. Alex said when she and her date got home at three a.m. "Call Beth and say you're sleeping on our couch." Beth was livid and insisted Dani come home.

Another time, Mrs. Alex returned so late from a hair

appointment that Dani arrived onstage partway through a Hawtones performance. Beth had invited her friends and was embarrassed. Mr. Gabler read Dani the riot act afterward.

"I know you can't leave a little kid alone," he said, "but you have to be resourceful and make other arrangements." He would give her another chance, he said, but if she missed part of a performance again she would be dropped from the group.

Dani began babysitting when her teammate Justine Lamont needed someone to take over for her one night. The next time, Justine simply didn't show up at the house, and Mrs. Alex called Dani. Justine told Dani she didn't want to sit for Alex anymore because the hours were so long and the house was so chaotic. This was just as well for Dani, because she had already fallen in love with Alex. Dani doesn't mind Mrs. Alex screwing up sometimes. She has a stressful job, and it can't be easy raising a kid by yourself.

"Why don't you bring him something next time you go over?" Beth asks Dani.

"What kind of something?"

"A present. A video game. I'll give you the money."

"Mrs. Alex makes good money, Mom. And I already got him a racket."

"Get him something from me. To cheer him up. It must be tough having a mother like that."

"Mom, I know you mean well, but it seems like your motivation for giving him a present is just to insult Mrs. Alex. If you want to give him something, do it because you like him, not as . . . as a consolation prize for having a crappy mom."

"I'm trying to help," Beth says. "I feel sorry for the little guy."

"I do too. But I like Mrs. Alex. She has an exciting life. She's kind of a free spirit. She's constantly going on dates." *Not like you, you dried-up twat!*

Oh no, Dani thinks.

Oh no. I was feeling good about having managed the lesbo *thing during the match, and now this new one pops up*. Dani's so tired of pushing thoughts away that she feels like crying. She can't go through this with Beth. She has to get Beth out of her room. She turns her chair away from the door.

"Mom, can I please have some time to myself? I want to learn this piece of music."

"All right. I'm going to do a little more cleaning. Sean is coming for dinner Thursday—will you be home?"

"I don't know yet."

Sean is Beth's boyfriend, who has a successful house-building company. Dani believes Beth is doing everything she can to get Sean to marry her, even though Sean has already been married three times and shows no sign of wanting to get married again. It's hard to know what's attractive about Sean, other than that he and Beth both have their own companies and can talk about work and buildings.

Every time Sean comes to dinner, Beth spends an hour cleaning in addition to what the cleaning service does. One night Beth lit candles all over the house, and Dani felt certain Beth was going to go for broke and propose to Sean herself. Dani told Beth she wasn't staying; she would sleep at Shelley's. After she left she realized she was embarrassed for her mother. When Dani came home the next morning, Sean was gone and Beth didn't let on that anything unusual had happened. She sat there listening to the news and eating a waffle. Dani toasted one too, although she had already had a bagel at Shelley's. She tried not to look at Beth. She felt terrible. She concentrated on squirting an equal amount of syrup into every square in the waffle, making a whole neighborhood of identical swimming pools.

"What will you wear if you stay home?" Beth lingers in the doorway with a Swiffer mop.

"I don't know if I'll be here."

"But if you do stay home, what do you think you'll wear?"

Who would want your dried-up old twat?

"Dani?"

You're all dried up, you old twat. No one would want to marry you!

Waiting for Dani's answer, Beth looks so hopeful and wistful and weak, she's trying so hard, that she seems like Alex. What if Dani yelled something that nasty, while her mother waits, blinking and vulnerable? In all their talks they have never discussed her mother's vagina. It seems excruciatingly personal. And Beth would be devastated about the Sean part. It might be the last nail in the coffin of her mother ever being happy. Dani tries to remember the last three things they said in this conversation. Did she really say *twat* or just think it? She touches her mouth to see if her lips are moving. *Please, Mom, please, get out of my room. Get out before I say something you don't want to hear.*

"Dani? What's wrong? Are you listening to me?"

"I'd wear this," Dani says, pointing to her ripped jeans and pink hoodie.

"You don't want to borrow something of mine?"

"I probably won't be home."

"Suit yourself," Beth says, going off to fine-tune the ambiance for Sean. Dani shuts the door. *Finally, she's gone. Thank God.*

Beth calls back from the hallway, "I like that song, Dani. Leave your door open so I can hear you practice."

10

"You were right about something," Malcolm Pinto tells his father during a break from yard work after school. They relax on lounge chairs on the back patio.

"What?"

"The jockette. You know, the tennis-playing one."

"Strawberry Shortcake's friend?"

"Yup. She is definitely a baby dyke."

Michael smiles. "How do you know for sure?"

"I heard them talking about it."

Michael peers at Malcolm over his sunglasses. "A lesbian in training." He takes a gulp from his soda. "Your old man knows the score."

"I guess so," Malcolm says. He folds one arm behind his head.

Malcolm's mom peeks out the door. "The lawn looks perfect," she says. "You're as good as the professionals."

Each week Malcolm and his father follow the same routine. They mow, then they trim the hedges and weed along the fence. Then Malcolm rakes while Michael uses the leaf blower. Mrs. Pinto talks on the phone while they work. She likes to brag to her friends about what a good crew she has. Afterward, father and son drive along the coast. Michael points at the girls running or Rollerblading along the beaches and breakwaters.

"There's one for ya," he tells Malcolm, once he's checked out a girl from both behind and the front. They stop at the beach shack for a burger and shake before heading home.

The work is done. Malcolm and Michael shower quickly and head to the Jeep for their drive. They pass the center of town. The coastline opens up before them. Malcolm imagines girls like Dani Solomon, Zoe Brightman, and Meghan Dimmock doing a double-take when he enrolls in the academy and starts running every day along the back shore.

"I wonder if Strawberry Shortcake's hair is natural," Malcolm muses.

"There's one way to be sure," his father says, grinning behind his shades.

"Look at her roots?" Malcolm guesses.

Michael smiles, taking his eyes off the road. Malcolm sees his reflection in his father's dark lenses, with wet, comb-marked hair and sunglasses of his own.

"Oh." Malcolm laughs, at the joke and at his own slowness. He feels he may never catch up.

11

On Wednesday, Dani hesitates at Alex's front steps. Why is she getting these pictures and words in her mind? Is she crazy? She's never been crazy before. She picks brown leaves off Mrs. Alex's geraniums. Under the welcome mat is a magazine subscription card that fell out of the mail. She picks it up. She dreads going inside. Now that she's started worrying about insulting Shelley and her mother, she's worried the thoughts about hurting Alex will come back.

Mrs. Alex rushes downstairs in scrubs and reptile-print heels. She grabs her lab coat and waves good-bye to Dani. Dani drops her backpack in the living room. She has three precalculus worksheets to complete.

"Give me a kiss," Alex says to Dani. "Do you know you're my favorite person?"

"I'm sure that's not true."

"It is."

"I bet your mom is your favorite."

"You're nicer than Mom." He pinches one knee of her cargo pants.

"Maybe today I'm your favorite. Maybe right now. But I bet Mrs. Alex is your favorite most of the time."

"You're nicer than her. She gets mad sometimes. You never get mad."

"Sometimes I do get mad. At my friends or people like that. But I wouldn't get mad in front of you. At least, I would try not to. For you I put on my special Alex face. I act my best, best, best. But I don't see you that much. Your mom sees you all the time, so she can't always have her best face on."

"Sometimes you do things that make me mad. But I put my good face on and don't tell you."

"Like what?"

"Like when you talk on your phone while you're here."

"To Shelley?"

"Yes."

"But I do that when you're asleep."

"I only pretend. I can still hear you."

"It bothers you when I talk to Shelley?"

"Yes."

"I have other friends, you know. You're not my only friend, Alex."

"Okay." He looks at the floor.

"You know how you have friends at school? I have friends at school too. Friends my own age. That's the way it's supposed to be. The more friends you have, the better off you are."

"Do you want to play with Louie?"

"I'm not sure I have time. Oh, all right. For a minute."

Dani sits at the computer with Alex on her knee. His rib cage feels as small around as a football. They play a game of picking blueberries and putting them in a bucket. Alex twists around.

"You're not watching Louie," he says.

Dani's staring at Mrs. Alex's *Venus de Milo* mousepad. The

pictures are in her mind again, of Alex lying on the floor, of her standing above him with a knife. She wonders if she could ever hurt a child, and what she can do to make sure that never happens.

"Sorry," she says. Alex hands her the mouse. The timer starts and Louie goes berry picking. She pictures herself standing over Alex's bed with a knife, waking him up and saying, "I'm going to kill you." She feels like there are two worlds, the one with Louie and the berries, and the one with Alex and Dani, in which everything has gone horribly wrong.

"Keep picking," Alex says. "You still have ten seconds."

The timer clicks. Louie's point score goes up. Soon Alex can redeem the points to furnish Louie's playroom. Dani looks in the fridge for dinner stuff. She orders pizza, salad, and soda for their supper, using the twenty bucks in her wallet.

Alex goes to bed and Dani starts her precalculus homework. She looks at her hands and rubs them. She checks on Alex to make sure he's still alive. She decides she must do something to prevent herself from possibly killing him. If, say, for instance, it's a quiet moment like this and Dani finds herself—without really wanting to but on some kind of autopilot—heading upstairs with a knife while Alex sleeps. She looks through Mrs. Alex's kitchen drawers to see if there are any knives that could kill someone. She finds three large knives, including a black-handled one that looks really deadly. She hides the knives in a box of crafts supplies in the garage. She locks the garage. She checks on Alex again. She unlocks the garage and puts the knives back in place ten minutes before Mrs. Alex comes home.

12

The next day in school, Dani's French teacher shows a film in which a boy is beaten by his father. This gets Dani thinking again about the guy who murdered his stepdaughter. His name, she knows by now, is Charles Bickie. Charles Bickie crossed a line, the line that separates nonmurderers from murderers. Once, for many days and many years, he was like her: a nonmurderer. But what he really was was a premurderer. His life was about to change—big time. She wonders if Charles Bickie stepped over that line by premeditated act or if he simply snapped. Dani tries to remember how Alex looked the last time she checked on him. She decides to call after school to make sure he's okay.

13

After calling Mrs. Alex ("He's fine. Why, was there a problem?"), Dani walks with Shelley to Icey's. The whole restaurant has been hijacked by a child's birthday party.

"Should we sit at the counter?" Dani asks.

"Let's wait," Shelley says. "Maybe a table will open up. Oh my God, look!"

In the corner beside the miniature igloo and fake fireplace is a discreet table that's ideal for whispered conversations, for hugging and kissing, or, if you want to get really crude, fondling and groping your date, although Dani has never groped anyone in the booth or been groped there. She's surprised to see Gordy sitting there talking to a guy in a tweed newsboy cap. But when Gordy and the guy wave, the guy turns out to be Meghan Dimmock.

"Oh my God!" Shelley says. "Oh no, oh no, oh no."

Several possibilities come to Dani's mind, raising their hands to volunteer for suckiest. One, that Gordy and Meghan are dating, which flashed through her mind once in practice when several people were out sick and Gordy and Meghan ended up massaging each other. Dani watched Meghan's fingers work their way down, lingering on each of Gordy's vertebrae. Then Gordy's fingers got down as far as her bra hooks and he gave her a pat and sent her on her way. Dani liked the fact that Gordy apparently had standards and boundaries. But now he's sitting in the corner booth beside Meghan's cleavage.

"I'm so sorry, Shell," Dani says.

"Hey, guys!" Meghan sopranos. In the cap she looks girly and boyish at the same time. "Come sit with us!"

Gordy waves his ice cream spoon at them. He would never yell with his mouth full.

"Do you want to?" Dani asks Shelley.

"We have to," Shelley says. "They already saw us. What can we do, turn around and walk out?"

Dani and Shelley link arms and walk to the booth together.

"You guys!" Meghan screams, hugging them. She's wearing plaid capris and a short, tight cardigan. A trace of her makeup sticks to Dani's face. It feels like it'll stay there forever, like the bits of glitter that get lost in the carpet.

Gordy hands them menus. "We're almost done, but you guys order whatever you want. Burgers, dinner, my treat." In addition to everything else excellent about Gordy, his dad is an important lawyer and gives him tons of spending money. Dani's mom works with lots of lawyers, but never with Mr. Abt, because he works only in Boston.

Meghan leans across the table and grabs one of Shelley's wrists and one of Dani's.

"Hey, you two. Do you think there'll be any scouts from *American Idol* at the end-of-year concert?"

"If I'm singing, the only scouts will be exit scouts," Shelley answers.

"Are you kidding?" Dani says. "You're an excellent musician."

"You are," Gordy agrees.

"Gordy and I were just talking about whether this group is the best showcase for my skills," says Meghan.

"You should do more singing on your own," Shelley says. "With just a piano. Torch songs."

Dani pulls back her wrist so she can hold the menu. "I'll just have ice cream. I can pay for my own."

"No, I insist," Gordy says. "Really, it's no problem."

He's paying and it's no problem, Dani thinks. So technically, if the other two weren't here, if he didn't appear to be seeing Meghan, and if we had arranged this in advance . . . if everything about this were different, it would be a date!

Shelley hasn't pulled away. A line of pink spreads from her chin to her bandanna. Dani wonders what Meghan's true deal is. Meghan might be the kind of straight girl who flirts with both sexes.

The food comes. Dani concentrates on eating her butterscotch sundae without dropping gooey stuff on the table.

Gordon tells how All-State band rehearsals were run compared to the way Mr. Gabler runs his. Meghan dips her spoon into his Heath bar ice cream and scoops up a dark spike of candy. "Mmm," she says.

Then Meghan feeds Gordy a spoonful of his own ice cream.

"Oopsh!" he says, surprised, trying to block the ice cream from his pale blue dress shirt.

"Let me clean you up," Meghan says, reaching for his face with her napkin.

Poor Shelley, Dani thinks. "Do you need us to leave?" Dani asks Meghan.

"No."

"Not at all," says Gordy.

A friend of Gordy's stops to say hi. "Let's go as soon as they're done," Dani whispers to Shelley while the others are talking.

"No way. This is an opportunity. We're staying right here."

Dani stirs her sundae until it turns beige. She feels a piercing romantic pain, but she'll stay for Shelley. Meghan aims a spoonful of Heath bar sundae at Shelley's mouth.

"Hey!" Gordy grabs Meghan's arm. "There won't be any left!"

"Isn't this getting unsanitary?" Dani asks.

Shelley opens her mouth, even though Dani knows Shelley only likes ice cream with fruit flavors. Dani thinks they'll always remember this, the day Shelley got her heart broken at Icey's.

Meghan, you skank! Why don't you and Shelley show everybody what lesbos do?

Oh God, please, Dani thinks. *Not here. Not now. No, please no. This is the worst possible time. Not with these three people. Not with Shelley. Not in front of Meghan. For God's sake, she's my best friend. Please go away, thoughts. You can come back another time.*

But the thoughts only get stronger. Dani imagines her own voice saying, *That's right, Shelley, you lesbo with your skank girlfriend! Why don't you put on a show for everybody?*

Did I say that in front of a child's birthday party? Dani touches her lips to see if they're moving.

Meghan sees Dani touching her lips. "Napkin, babe?" She

zooms in with the same napkin she's been using on Gordy and Shelley.

Lesbo, lesbo, skank, skank!

How could I even think that? Dani wonders. *Okay, I do think Meghan is kind of cheap, but I would never say that in front of Shelley. It would hurt Shelley to the quick and I know she'd be furious at me. And what difference does my opinion of Meghan make, anyway? Meghan doesn't need to know what I think of her. And that lesbo thing, I don't believe it's wrong; I know I don't. It doesn't matter to me if Shelley is gay or straight. She's just Shelley. I've looked deep inside myself and I truly don't believe I'm homophobic. But then why would I even think that? Does it mean I am bigoted? I can't stay here. I'm about to ruin everything for Shelley.*

Dani grabs her pack from under the table. "I gotta get up," she tells Shelley. She watches Shelley for a reaction to any homophobic remarks she may have made.

"Dude, we just sat down," Shelley says.

"Bathroom?" Meghan asks. "I'll come with you, *chiquita*."

"Gotta get home," Dani says. "My mom's making a special dinner."

"Uh-oh," Gordy says. "Somebody ate dessert before dinner. Stay and finish. We won't tell."

"Don't bail on me now," Shelley says. She grabs the edge of Dani's sweatshirt. "The four of us have so much to talk about. Maybe we can mutiny and take the Hawtones in a whole new direction."

"What time will you be done with dinner?" Gordy asks. "We can all drive around in my car and practice together."

"I mean it, Dani," Shelley whispers. "Don't bail on me now. You hate those dinners. Call Bethie and say you can't come."

"I need to go," Dani says. "Thank you for the ice cream."

Gordy stands up while Dani gets out of the booth. "You're welcome. I'm sorry you couldn't stay. Maybe I can buy you dinner sometime. Somewhere nicer than this."

"It was very nice," she says, hardly hearing him. Dani hurries past the parents of the birthday child, who stand by patiently, crunching gift paper into an open bag. She can't wait to get outside, away from children and friends and anyone else who could get hurt.

14

"Call me this second," says the text message.

Dani waits for the right moment to excuse herself.

"Why don't we have our coffee in the living room?" Beth asks. Dani knows this means Sean and not her.

Sean gets up. "Wonderful, Beth. I better be careful or you'll fatten me up." He pats his stomach. Unlike Dani's mom, who often jumps on the elliptical trainer after a long day selling real estate, Sean doesn't take good care of his body. But Dani's mom doesn't care. She thinks Sean is desirable to every woman he meets. "He's so good-looking," Beth often says, tapping the computer screen after posting pictures of the latest real estate party. "Isn't he?"

"I'll clear, Mom. That was delicious, thanks." Dani removes the rack of lamb and the bowl of herbed potatoes. Her phone vibrates again. "Where are you? Need to talk to you. You will not believe this." Her mother goes into the living room with espresso and a tray of cookies.

"What, what, what?" Dani says to Shelley.

"Hi," Shelley says. Then a long pause.

"What? 'Call me, call me, I need to talk,' and now you're not saying anything?"

"I can't talk. It's too amazing."

"What is?"

"It's too amazing to even say."

"Is this about what happened at Icey's?"

"Meghan and I are going to a movie."

"When?"

"Probably Saturday. She has to check about something else. It'll be a long wait."

"How did this happen?"

"I asked her when the three of us were leaving Icey's, and she said yes!"

"The three of you? Gordy was still there too?"

"Yep. We all left together."

"Was it weird asking in front of him?"

"I was pretty cool about it. You should have seen me. I wish you had stayed!"

"Sorry, I just started feeling really uncomfortable."

"It was the best time! You should have stayed."

"I can't believe you're seeing a movie with Meghan Dimmock."

"I said, 'Hey, do you want to hang out sometime, maybe go to a movie?' Really low-key."

Dani carries the dirty silverware from the dining room to the dishwasher.

"Can anybody hear you?" Shelley asks.

"Nobody's listening. They're in the living room. Sean is eating hundreds of tiny cookies. Where are you?"

"Home. Almost home. You're still the only one I've told. That knows me, that is. I'm in a couple of chat rooms, but no one there knows who I am. Don't tell anyone, okay?"

"Of course not. I have not told anyone and I absolutely swear that I'll never tell anyone."

"Okay. I just get really nervous about it."

Dani tries to imagine being Shelley. She wonders if the secrecy takes some fun out of parts of being young, such as falling in love, or if the secrecy makes falling in love more special, more sacred.

"You're brave, you know that?" Dani says.

Nothing on Shelley's end for a minute. Then, "I guess you're right," she says.

15

Later that night, Beth's office phone rings. The display says GORDON ABT.

"I'll get it, Mom," says Dani.

"Um, hi. Hello?" comes the voice at the other end.

"Hi," says Dani.

"It's Gordon. I hope you don't mind that I'm calling."

"No, I don't mind. Did Shelley give you this number?"

"I got it from the phone book."

"Right. My mother's number," Dani says. "That's no problem." Duh. Why is she saying "no problem"? Has he thanked her for something? No. Is his call inconvenient? No. Is she implying that using her mother's number violated her privacy? She isn't making much sense. But she's still reacting to seeing that name on the screen. Beth and Sean are still in the living room.

"It was cool running into you at Icey's. I wish you could have stayed."

Why? Dani wants to ask. But she says, "Thank you again for the ice cream. Sorry I had to rush off."

"There's something I wanted to ask you, though I couldn't say it in front of the other two."

What could that be, since you're dating Meghan?

"I think it would be cool if we learned the new songs together.

Or even if we practiced together as a regular thing. I mean, since you support the soloist and I do the rhythm line."

"Wow," Dani replies. "That would be great." She reaches for her cell phone. She's going to text this to Shelley: !!!!!!!!!!!!!

"You sound hesitant."

I do? I thought I sounded too eager. "No, really," Dani says. "I would like to. I mean it. It would help us learn the music and it would be kind of . . . fun."

"Okay, then. My house all right? I have a keyboard at home, plus I have a MIDI player we can run the music through. But your sightreading seems pretty good."

"I can tell whether the notes go up or down," Dani says, although actually she does more than that.

"Me too," Gordy says.

"I guess so, Mr. All-State!" Dani never teased Gordy before. The intensity of her crush made every conversation deathly serious. At night she reviewed everything they said to each other, sifting each conversation for stupidity and errors, like a gold miner in reverse. Now his having called makes her feel light, as if a rainy, fast-drying road is opening up in front of them.

"I had a lot of music classes where I lived before I came here," Gordy tells her. "Private lessons, too. My mom thought music was really important."

"So this rehearsal concept of yours," Dani says. "When would it start?"

"How about tomorrow?"

"I have to babysit."

"Tuesday?"

"Sure," Dani says. Mrs. Alex doesn't work that day. "Well, thanks for calling. I'll be looking forward to that."

"Wait! Can we talk for a few minutes?"

"Sure." *Ugh, I'm acting so awkward. He's going to think nobody ever calls me.*

"So do you enjoy being in Hawtones, or do you view it as more of a résumé builder?"

"A little of both. I wish the song selections were better."

"What do you like most about being in the group?"

"I could ask you the same question."

"Should I tell you?"

"Sure, if you want."

"With my horn playing, I don't really need another music activity on my transcript. I keep going to rehearsal because I like knowing that I'll see you."

"Really?" Even though her heart had vaulted like a gymnast at seeing his name on the caller ID, Dani hadn't expected anything like this.

"I enjoy it mostly because of you," he repeats. "So."

"Am I supposed to be playing hard-to-get here?" Dani asks.

"Not necessarily."

"I enjoy going to rehearsal for the same reason. But what about Meghan?"

"You mean at Icey's?"

"I guess I made other assumptions. Sharing the ice cream."

"I admit I played that up a little. I was looking for an indication from you. A sign."

"You're giving me a lot to think about," Dani says. "I sort of want to hang up so I can go away and think about it. Is that insulting?"

"Not really. I understand how you feel."

"So."

"Want to both hang up?" Gordon asks. "Even though it would be impolite?"

"Sure."

"Let's not even say good-bye."

"No, let's not. In fact, the person who hangs up quicker is showing how much they need to go away and think about—"

16

Now Dani's so high, nothing can bring her down.

It's me! It's me! It's not Meghan, It's me! The sublime coincidence of the person she likes very much liking her very much back. What were the chances of that?

He's mine!

She's on time for Alex the next day. She challenges him to ten footraces around the block. Afterward, they go online and play with Louie. Dani's phone rings. She tries not to answer it when she's with Alex in case he's mad or sad that he's not getting her full attention. But Gordy has her cell number now, so she has to at least check. It's Shelley, announcing that she talked to Meghan one minute ago.

"It's weird to be on the phone with Meghan," Shelley says. "To hear her voice but not see her at the same time. I don't know which I like better, her face or her voice."

"Well, guess who called me last night."

"You're kidding. That's why the exclamation points?"

"We're rehearsing together."

"Rehearsing? Are you really rehearsing, or is it like . . . a thing?"

"It's a definite thing. What's going on with Meghan?"

"I . . . don't . . . know. Hmm." It's an old Shelley habit. The more excited she is about something, the more she wants the other person to drag it out of her. But Dani really should give the time to Shelley, because Dani's had crushes before that they talked about lots. There was Joshua Sandy, whom she kayaked out to the float with every night at summer camp. And Alan Diaz, whom she started dating when his family was already planning to move to Washington, DC. But Shelley has never had a girlfriend to talk about—at least, not officially.

"I don't know," Shelley says. "I'm going to become her friend and see if anything develops. That's the mature way, right? But . . ." She pauses again, waiting for Dani to prod her with questions.

"But what?"

"But if I want to be more and she doesn't, I don't know if I can deal with it. I mean I'm excited about getting to know her, but I don't know how much I should stick my neck out."

Alex clicks the mouse loudly.

Not at all, Dani thinks. She wants to warn Shelley to be careful, but she doesn't want to seem too critical of Meghan. So she can't say anything. Dani wonders how many times she'll go through that circle of thoughts, over and over. She wants to say, "I would hate to see you get hurt," but then couldn't Shelley say the same thing to her? Any time you really like someone and let them know it, you run the risk of getting hurt.

Alex thumps Dani's leg with the soles of his sneakers. When she says "Ow!" he looks the other way as if it was an accident. His sneakers have lights that flash when his feet move.

"I have to go," she tells Shelley. "I'm on the clock. I should feed my friend here."

"You're so conscientious. When I babysit my brother I barely look at him all night. I have him trained to heat Hot Pockets for both of us."

"You're not getting paid."

"Not directly, no."

"Indirectly?"

"I use babysitting to blackmail my parents when I want to stay out late."

"This weekend should have some staying-out-late opportunities."

"So where are you and Gordy rehearsing?"

"Oh, stop it! What's with that tone?" But Dani's smiling. She's grateful that Shelley brought Gordy up again. Maybe her relationship is not so rare, so hidden, so one-of-a-kind, but still, it's hers, her personal feeling that should not be scoffed at or broken, that she clutches like her own baby bird egg.

"Yeah, right, rehearsing. He is pretty hot."

"Well, it sounded really innocent. He has this old-fashioned niceness about him . . ."

"So where?"

"His house."

"Everyone says his dad is rich. A lot of his customers, whatever you call them—"

"Clients."

"Are musicians, like really famous ones."

"That's what my mom says. But look, I should probably—ow."

"I'll let you go then, little mommy. God, you're such a Girl Scout.

I'd go crazy putting in the hours you do. See you in class, okay?"

"Okay. Bye.

"What?" Dani says, realizing she hasn't heard Alex.

"We bought Louie a hockey stick. It's in his toy box."

"Oh."

Alex grasps her ears and presses his nose against hers, turning into a cyclops.

"You look funny," he says. "You're my favorite person in the world."

Dani's mind starts to go to the bad place again. She had thought that wouldn't happen today, because she was so happy. But then Shelley said how good Dani was, and Dani felt bad because Shelley had no idea what Dani sometimes thought about when she came to this house.

Yes, her mind is going to that place again, even though when she arrived she was a normal, dopey girl falling in love. She wonders if she's on the verge of something happening. She pictures Alex's face, this face that's pressed against her, all over the TV and the newspapers. His darling face. Oh God, she couldn't bear it. If precious, adorable Alex were dead, and if she were the one who killed him . . . What would the headlines say?

MAYHEM IN HAWTHORNE HOME

SITTER STABS TOT

POLICE: TEEN WENT "BERSERK"

EMTS: "IT WAS A BLOODBATH"

NEIGHBOR: "WHO COULD HARM AN ANGEL?"

Dani's heart starts to pound. All the details are so real. It feels like it could happen. It feels like it might happen. Except that she doesn't want to kill Alex. So why does she keep picturing his death?

"You're my favorite," he says again.

"Don't say that, Alex," Dani says. She scoots out from under him, off the chair. "I'll start dinner."

"Okay," he says, meaning it isn't okay. He scowls and drops his head on the keyboard, careful not to hit any keys.

She leaves him alone and finds chicken tenders in the fridge and a can of corn on the pantry shelf. Why does Mrs. Alex keep buying corn if Alex doesn't eat it? *I'll have to bribe him to eat this,* she thinks. She hopes there are Popsicles. Unless Alex is already dead. Is it possible that she already killed Alex but forgot? Did she go into some kind of trance she has no memory of? And is he lying on the floor right now? That's impossible, right? Or is it?

She checks the living room. Alex is alive, arranging his plastic animals in a circle around the ottoman.

He scowls. "Are you done yet?"

"Back in a minute," she says.

All she wants is to protect him. *Who would want to kill such a great kid?* she asks, echoing the neighbor in the imaginary news headline. She finds the three big knives and puts them in the craft box and locks the garage. *Enough craziness,* she decides. *I need to tell somebody.*

part 2 LINES AND CIRCLES

17

"How hard would it be to find another sitter?" Dani asks Mrs. Alex that night. "I mean, if I had other commitments?" Dani tries to sound causal, but desperation tightens her face.

"What other commitments do you have?" Mrs. Alex asks. She pries off her heels in the front hall. "Is somebody offering you more money?" She tries to sound casual too, as if nothing is at stake, although Dani knows she must be surprised and hurt.

"It's not that. Just . . . school and stuff."

Mrs. Alex straightens. Without her shoes, she's four inches shorter than Dani. "All right, Dani. I won't lie to you. It would be difficult. You would be hard to replace."

Come on, come on, get me out of here, Dani's mind says. *Come on, it can't be that difficult.* She tries not to look impatient.

"I guess I should be flattered," Dani says. It seems the perfect thing to say, balancing kindness and persistence. "I am flattered. But maybe if I could find a replacement—a friend from tennis, or someone else at school . . ."

"I could find someone, sure, but not anyone that Alex likes as much as you—that we both like as much as you. Who could deal with my disorganization? And you've never said one thing about it."

"It's not so bad."

"Are you looking for a raise? Is that it?" She looks the way Dani's mother looks when she starts to talk about money. They're single women who don't want people putting one over on them.

"No, I don't need a raise."

"We might be getting an increase at work. If I do, you'll get an automatic increase, too. How does that sound?" Mrs. Alex hangs her cell phone holder, keys, and work ID on pegs inside the door. She's trying to become more organized. She buys books about organizing. But things stay put for only a day or two before joining the disorder. Dani can almost hear the disorder churning, like the rotating bin on a garbage truck.

Dani nearly laughs. The money's not it. She can get money anytime she wants from her mom. Dani would almost pay Mrs. Alex to let her go, no more questions asked, no cajoling or convincing. But she can't think of another tactic.

"I don't know what I'm talking about. It was just a hypothetical."

"You look really tired, sweetheart," Mrs. Alex says. "I've never seen you so wiped out. School okay? Not too much partying? It takes one to know one, you know. Want a ride home? It's so late."

"I'd rather walk and clear my head. I have my phone. I'll tell my mom I'm en route." Dani picks up her bag.

"You wouldn't quit without giving me plenty of notice, would you?"

"I don't know if I will quit. It sounds like you need me not to."

"I do. And it would kill Alex."

It would kill Alex. How casually people said awful, terrible things. Her leaving wouldn't kill Alex. But it would mess up his life. And Mrs. Alex's, too.

How long will this go on? Dani wonders. Dani had walked around the house with her hands squeezed together. She had checked on Alex ten or twelve times, locked up the knives, put them back before Mrs. Alex came home, and changed the TV channel every time something nasty came on. In the last ten minutes she felt a huge sense of relief, because Mrs. Alex would be home and Dani would be glad to see her, to tell her everything's all right, to sign off on Alex, and to quit and never spend a night like this again.

18

"Hey, Shell. Do you ever have . . . weird thoughts?" Dani asks. They're eating lunch in the courtyard.

"My whole life is one weird thought," Shelley says. She offers Dani shoestring potatoes and a tub of tuna salad. "Isn't everybody's?"

"No, I mean icky weird thoughts. Something bizarre and random that you wouldn't want to think of."

"Here's an unexpected thought, Dani: I have no idea what you're talking about."

A bump in the road. But Dani is prepared. She knew she would have to work up to this conversation. She psyched herself up during biology lab while staining slides with Jess Blodgett. *I'm going to talk to my best friend,* Dani told herself. *I will sit down with my best friend and tell her what's bothering me, and see what she thinks.*

Dani dips a potato in the tuna. She chews as if a new idea has captured her mind and she's deciding what to say next. But in fact she rehearsed every word.

"I mean, you get a thought about something you might do . . ." Chew, chew, swallow. "Then you wonder, Oh my God, what if one day I really did that? What if I couldn't help myself?"

Shelley swats an ant off the leg of her jeans. "For example?"

Dani leans on one elbow. She makes herself smile like she's saying something ridiculous.

"Like when we're rehearsing and Mr. Gabler is standing there teaching us our parts and jabbering on about something, do you ever get the urge to reach out and grab his testicles?"

"Ew! EEEEEEW!" Shelley nearly spits her potatoes. She stares at Dani with her mouth open, the way someone looks hanging over the toilet after throwing up. Then she yells again.

"Ew! Ew! Mr. Gabler's?"

"Mr. Gabler's testicles," Dani says. She still hopes that this can go her way.

"Don't say that! Don't say that! Don't say that!"

"Somehow I didn't expect such a strong reaction." Dani can barely hear herself through the yelling.

"Ew! Ew!" Shelley drops the can of potatoes on the ground and shakes her hands around her head in a shivery way, like she's touched something contaminated.

"Please don't scream just because I mentioned Mr. Gabler's testicles."

"Aaaah! You keep saying it. Do not say 'Mr. Gabler' and 'testicles' in the same sentence. Not even in the same conversation! In the same life! In the same world!"

"But I mean, you know how he wears those pants that are that shiny material, nylon or polyester or something, and in some places they're really worn out, and you can see the outline of . . ."

"I know, Dani. I know. I've seen it. And I don't want to think about it! Now shut up. That is nasty."

"Okay, it is nasty. I agree with you."

Dani lays down her food and squeezes her hands together.

Other kids in the yard have stopped talking and are watching Dani and Shelley. Malcolm Pinto leans against the wall by the plants, picking tobacco from his teeth.

"That's right," Shelley says. "Now look around. Everyone's staring at us."

"No, they're just staring at you. Could you please keep your voice down?"

"Ew! Ew! Now I can't eat." Shelley jams the potatoes and tuna into her backpack. She purses her lips and stares at Dani for a minute, sizing her up. "So, now that the cat's out of the bag, have you had weird thoughts about any of our other teachers? Ms. Martin, for example, or Dr. Chang? Do you want to grab any part of them?"

"Not really." Dani laughs.

"'Cause I sure don't!"

"But now that you put the idea in my head, maybe I will."

"Well, if you're going to subject them to an undies critique, why don't you hit Ms. Martin next? I sometimes find myself transfixed by that, you know, uniboob of hers."

"I think I know what you mean," Dani says. "One, where there should be two. Can you open those potatoes again?"

Shelley makes a face like she's been hypnotized. "Maybe you could get a weird thought or urge, before she walks into the classroom, to write on the board 'Buy a new bra.'"

"Or what about over on the side where she writes the vocabulary words for the day? I could get an urge to add 'lift' and 'separate.'" Dani plays along, even though Shelley's making fun of her.

"Mr. Gabler, huh?" Shelley muses. "You have the hots for him."

Dani notices that the other kids stopped paying attention when she joined the joking. They seemed to have a sixth sense for the truth, a focus on the moment when Dani was most uncomfortable. So she backed off the subject. But she has gotten nowhere, and now she'll have to start over.

"No, I don't have the hots for him." She holds the potatoes far from Shelley until Shelley looks apologetic.

"Oh God, Dani. Now I have this totally unwanted image of Mr. Gabler in my mind, thanks to you. I don't know how I can get through rehearsal next time. I'll keep thinking about . . . what you said."

"I'm sorry," Dani says. "I know it's weird, but I thought . . . I thought you might relate."

"Well, I honestly don't relate. I don't at all."

Dani finishes the tuna while Shelley watches the other kids. "Peanut butter cookie?" Dani asks, taking a foil-wrapped package from her knapsack. "With chocolate pudding? They're homemade by Beth."

"Maybe later. Save one for me."

"Okay," Dani says. "I'll surprise you and put one in your locker. Hey, let me ask you something else. Do you ever find yourself thinking, for no particular reason, about hurting another person?" She squeezes her hands again. She doesn't know whether to adopt a light tone or to sound serious.

Shelley positions her pack as a pillow. "Someone you're mad at? Do what we did in summer camp. Covertly feed the object of your hatred an entire package of Ex-Lax."

"But I don't think I really am mad at the person, see?"

"Ex-Lax completely leaves the system within twenty-four hours."

Shelley stretches on the bench with one hand resting on her abdomen. Since she started texting Meghan all the time, she seems to move differently. Shelley has a really solid body. Malcolm is staring again.

"I mean, what if you didn't want to hurt them at all?" Dani says. "If you just thought about it?"

"Then make an effigy and stick pins in it. Safe, fun, and cathartic. And if anything bad does befall this person, hey, it's probably a coincidence."

Dani dips a cookie into the pudding. "Hey, do me a favor, girlfriend?" she asks. "Don't tell anyone what we just talked about. I feel like such a jerk."

"Two peanut butter cookies."

"Deal."

"What conversation?" Shelley says. "It never happened."

19

"I heard something weird today and I don't know what to make of it." Malcolm and his dad are driving to their favorite hardware store to look at grills for Father's Day.

"What's that, son?"

"It's about Strawberry Shortcake."

"What's that little cutie up to?"

"She told Baby Dyke she had an urge to grab the music teacher. Mr. Gabler."

"Grab him how?"

"I'll let you guess. Hint: There are two of them."

"Not his twins? His boys?" Michael lowers his sunglasses and peers at Malcolm.

"That's right."

"Wow," Michael says, stopping at a traffic rotary and tapping the wheel. "Let me digest that for a second."

"I was kinda surprised. Did you ever hear of a girl getting the urge to grab a guy's nuts?"

"Not since I married your mother."

Malcolm laughs and nearly drops his soda, although the joke makes him a little uncomfortable. No matter how funny his dad is, Malcolm doesn't feel entirely right hearing intimate sex things about his mother.

"Gotcha," Michael says, handing his son a wad of napkins. "A beautiful young girl like that wanting to grab the teacher's jewels? I knew I went into the wrong line of work." He looks to see if he got another laugh. "Do you think this teacher and Strawberry Shortcake are having some kind of affair? That might be legal, depending on her age, but it would be unethical. I would want to report that. He would lose his job."

"I don't imagine so. He's kind of your average middle-aged guy. He looks kind of like a eunuch."

"She was joking, then," Michael says.

"Not entirely. That's why it seemed weird. She looked all riled up, like she really was going to molest this dorky teacher. A Jekyll-and-Hyde situation, maybe?"

Michael pulls into the store parking lot. "I have one further explanation. I call it the one-size-fits-all explanation, and it's very simple."

"Meaning?"

"All that glitters is usually not gold, son. Your comely friend Strawberry Shortcake is apparently wackier than a bag of hammers."

"Nuttier than rat shit in a pistachio factory?" Malcolm asks, using another expression his father taught him.

"You want to watch out for girls like that," Michael says, opening the door to the store. "Girls like Strawberry Nutcake."

20

Beth Solomon moved the dining room chairs into the living room, pushed the table aside, and covered it with an old sheet. Now she's at the top of a step stool in last year's capris and a ball cap to protect her hair.

"When will you be done?" Dani asks. This time she's intent on getting it right, telling about the weird thoughts. She's going to start serious and keep it serious. She's not going to let the conversation become screamingly funny, as apparently happened with Shelley and Mr. Gabler's testicles. She's not leaving this room until her mother knows what's been happening.

"Probably an hour and a half. I'm not too happy with the job I'm doing. I'd rather work by natural light. This electric lamp is casting shadows and I know I'm missing a few spots."

"But if the old paint is white and the new paint is white, what difference does it make?"

Beth scratches her nose, then checks her hand too late to see if there's paint on it. "It's a different shade of white. What do you say on Saturday you help me do the ceiling in your room?"

Beth had her own real estate firm by age thirty and was the best-selling broker in Hawthorne. Lately she's said the money from selling houses is chicken feed and she might start selling office buildings. But she still likes houses a lot. She can afford to hire painters and she knows the best ones, but she says she finds painting relaxing. Once Dani heard Beth tell their neighbor Lynette that when she touched all the walls with her own hands she felt like she was making love to her house.

"I have no complaints about that ceiling," Dani says.

"That's because you're never home." A drip forms at the edge of the roller. Beth smushes the drippy edge against the ceiling.

"Mom, I'm asking when you'll be done because I need to talk."

"You do?" She places her wet roller in the paint pan and climbs down. She appears concerned but also excited—she and Dani haven't had a good mother-daughter talk in a while. "Should I make us some tea?"

"No, thanks," Dani says. "Let's talk here, like this."

Now that she's built up some momentum, Dani wants to keep going. On her way home Dani rehearsed what she would say to her mother. She decided that when she spoke to her mom she would use the word *hurt* early on, but to prevent her mother from panicking, she would not use the words *stab* or *kill*.

"Mom," she begins, "do you ever worry that you'll lose control?"

"What do you mean, with men?"

Dani takes a rag and wipes the paint from Beth's nose. In a world full of nasty events, her mother can think of only one way things can go wrong.

"I mean, do you ever worry that you'll hurt someone, that you'll get this urge to do the wrong thing and it will happen without your controlling it and later everything will be awful and the whole world will be ruined?"

"I used to."

"You did?"

Beth puts on the old eyeglasses that are hanging around her neck. "When I started in the business, I stayed awake nights worrying that I had snapped at someone or poached on somebody's turf or moved too quickly or hurt someone's feelings. I thought I was making a bad impression and it was all going to come back to me in the end. I agonized over those things. But eventually I saw that I kept getting calls and people seemed to like working with me, so I figured I was doing okay. I'm not sure we should all worry about that stuff as much as we do. Other people can take care of themselves. We don't have to be overprotective. It's up to us to take care of ourselves."

"Right," Dani says. She has that feeling, like a premonition, that a line exists between the real world and the world inside her mind, and that someday she will cross the line and the two worlds will become one. Her mother is so innocent and naive, with her freckle phobia and business ethics and paint colors. At the same moment that her mother says "Don't be overprotective," Dani feels that she needs to protect her. But then she gets an image of Beth being up on the ladder. In her mind, Dani knocks over the ladder by nudging it with her shoulder. Her mother falls, her head strikes the table. Blood seeps from her reddish-blond hair into the ball cap and overwhelms the smell of paint and Beth's avocado-cucumber skin lotion. What does blood smell like? Dani's heart pounds and she feels unsteady. Dani folds her hands in front of her like an old-fashioned girl in an old picture. She squeezes her hands to make sure she isn't touching the ladder. She has already said *hurt*. How can she explain what she means without saying *stab* or *kill*?

"Do you feel all right, Dani?" Beth asks. She comes closer. Dani ruffles her mother's hair to see if there's blood on her scalp.

"What's that, paint?" Beth says. "I'm such a slob when I do this. I just love getting my hands dirty."

Dani squeezes the rag between her hands. "I guess I'll go to bed," she tells Beth. Dani has noticed that when she's babysitting, if she gets sleepy she doesn't have the thoughts. Maybe she'll go to her room and pick the most boring music or TV show. Sleep will get her away from Mom and the ladder.

"So early? No tea?"

"Not tonight."

Beth checks her arm for paint and presses it around Dani, a partial hug. "How do you like my advice? Did I answer your question?"

Dani can't imagine talking about what's really on her mind. "I guess," she says.

"Are you resting enough? Have you been staying up too late? Is there a boy? Who have you been texting lately?"

"There is someone," Dani admits.

"Is he the one you're worried about hurting?"

"That's not what I meant," Dani says. She goes to her room and puts something droney on the music player. For an hour the images persist: her mother, Alex, Mrs. Alex. *It's hopeless,* she thinks. *It's all hopeless*. Then she squeezes her hands and thinks, *But at least I'm not hurting anyone.* Her hands part when she falls asleep.

21

"You're a really nice girl," Gordy says. "I'm totally impressed with you."

"I don't know. Maybe not so nice."

Gordy takes her hand. They practiced for a couple hours at his house before he suggested a walk in Havenswood. It's a perfect May evening, and they're going to climb a granite boulder called Shark's Jaw to watch the sunset.

Dani's house is big, but Gordy's is bigger. His father has a dark green office with glass-fronted bookcases, photos of famous musician clients, and a collection of vinyl records. Gordy showed Dani his computer software that scans sheet music and plays the notes.

Gordy was at the computer and as she stood over him, she could barely resist kissing the top of his head. She's wearing skinny dark-wash jeans, a white T-shirt with a sweetheart neck, and a pearl hair clip. He complimented her singing voice, her sightreading skills, and her positive attitude in the Hawtones, and he told her she was beautiful. Now on their walk to the boulder his hand feels strong and confident, like the hands of girl tennis players from other schools when Dani congratulates them after a match.

"So you're not nice?" Gordy repeats. "In what way are you not nice? I know. You're an ax murderer and you have bodies piled up in your basement."

"Stop," Dani says. Just when things were going so well. His joke opens a curtain on a scene: an ax, a basement, parts of Gordy beside other parts they shouldn't be beside. She doesn't want to have those thoughts. She's enjoying the walk and doesn't want to rush away. She wants to watch the sunset, not go home and will herself to sleep.

"Come on, tell me the bad news," Gordy says, tugging her hand so she faces him. "Am I your next victim?"

"Knock it off. I mean it." She drops his hand and walks ahead.

"Hey, come back. I'm sorry. I was kidding around. I know, it was gross."

Dani turns around. "We don't even have a basement."

"All right, so let's get back to you not being nice. Does that mean you're nasty?"

"Cut it out." This is better. She acts huffy but smiles.

"In what way are you nasty? Do you swear too much? Do you cut ahead in the lunch line? Are your library books overdue?"

"None of the above."

Gordy catches up with her. "Press one for more options? I have it: You once stole a dollar from the tip cup at Starbucks! I guessed your secret."

Dani squeezes her hands together. *I'm not hurting anyone.* She gazes at the top tree branches with their soft, green May buds and she breathes out like a smoker exhaling a long plume.

"Hey, what's wrong?"

"I guess I'm in a serious mood."

They start walking again.

"I know why you're upset," he says. "I should know better by now."

"What do you mean?"

"The way I talk to girls sometimes. With the Starbucks and the library books. Like they're so different from boys. Innocent. Dainty. One girl I dated called me patronizing."

"Forget it."

"I wouldn't patronize you, Dani."

"Let's be quiet for a while. Let's enjoy the sounds of nature."

Gordy listens. "The wind in the leaves, the birds," he says. "Do you think that's where people got the idea of creating music, or do you think it came from somewhere else? I don't usually talk this much. I don't know what's happening to me."

Something runs parallel to them before burrowing into the leaves.

"Chipmunk," Gordy says.

"Wow."

"I wasn't raised that way, you know."

"What way?"

"To patronize girls. Neither of my parents tolerated sexism. And my mom, my mom—"

What everyone in Hawthorne knows about Gordy is that his mom died after they moved to town. She was a lawyer too, like his dad. She signed Gordy up for school while coughing blood into a handkerchief. Dani thinks how awful it would be for his father to go through that and then to find Gordy hacked into pieces in their basement.

"The sun's almost setting," she says. She breaks into a run. He's beside her. They're evenly matched.

"Long legs," he says, but he's complimented her so much she can't hear it anymore; all she knows is she's having fun again.

At the base of Shark's Jaw, Dani crosses the path to Gordy's side. They're both panting. She places her hand against the back of his head, pressing his forehead against her shoulder. She ruffles his hair and checks his scalp for signs of blood. *He's okay*, she thinks. *I'm not hurting anyone.*

"That felt nice," he says. "What you just did. You are nice. I know you are. I can feel it."

The charge from practicing in his house is still between them, but broken down outdoors and softened, and it passes easily from her to him and back again. He wears a white T-shirt too, so she feels like they're brother and sister, or twin babies.

"Time to climb up," he says.

"Wait," says Dani. Her hands drift down to the belt loops of his jeans. "I want to ask you something."

"You want me to pay your overdue fines? No way!"

"No." She brushes away the joke and presses her cheek into his so he can't see her expression. "Gordon, have you ever worried that you would hurt someone who trusts you, someone who's vulnerable?"

"Dani," he says, turning her face to him, "I don't care if you end up hurting me. You can do your worst as far as I'm concerned. Because between now and then, it's going to be great. It's going to be spectacular."

22

Dani hates having bad thoughts about Gordy, Shelley, Mrs. Alex, Beth, and Mr. Gabler. But it's worse having bad thoughts about Alex. If Dani lost control with a friend or an adult, he or she could fight back, but Alex couldn't. She would be alone with him, and no one would protect him against Dani.

She calls Mrs. Alex and leaves a message: "I need to talk to you about the job. I need to talk to you about babysitting."

23

Dani rings the bell. *No stab or kill*, she tells herself. You need to have this conversation without using the words *stab* or *kill*.

Alex appears inside the screen door.

"You're not coming till tomorrow," he says.

"I know. But I need to talk to your mom. I wasn't able to get her on the phone. I left a ton of messages saying I need to talk, but she hasn't called me back."

Dani's babbling. Alex doesn't need to know all this. He doesn't care about phone messages. But she keeps talking because he's the person she owes an apology to. He's the most important one, not her or Mrs. Alex. His voice was on the recording when she called Mrs. Alex and left a message. His voice stopping and starting while Mrs. Alex, in the background, told him what to say and when to go ahead. *How will I tell him I'm finished and I'm not coming back?*

Dani couldn't get Mrs. Alex to call her back. She had called the house line three times and Mrs. Alex's cell phone twice. She had even paged the cell phone and called Mrs. Alex at work. She kept calling, kept making it sound important. "I need to talk to you about the job . . ." "I need to talk to you about babysitting . . ." "I need to talk to you about Alex . . ." She even said, "I'm worried about Alex . . . ," but Mrs. Alex didn't call her back. Now she has to get her attention but carefully. Sensitively. Without using the words *stab* or *kill*.

"We made you something," Alex tells her. "It's for tomorrow, when you come over."

"You did?"

"Hi," Mrs. Alex says, opening the door. She's wearing the yoga pants and slippers that say "comfy day at home." "I didn't think I'd see you until tomorrow."

"Didn't you get my messages?" All in all, there had been seven.

"I did. I just thought it would be best if we talked in person."

"That's why I'm here."

"If we talked in person next time we saw each other."

"Here it is," Alex says, pulling her to the couch and climbing on her lap. He gives her a certificate made from a computer template. At the top are the words WORLD'S BEST BABYSITTER, with her name underneath. Under that it says, "The only person who can deal with the chaos of our household and always come through smiling." A piece of clip art shows a teenage girl with eight arms feeding a baby, playing Ping-Pong with another child, doing her homework, putting a pizza in the oven, talking on the phone, bathing a dog, and vacuuming pet hair from the floor. The certificate is signed by Alex and Mrs. Alex. Alex prefers to sign his name Ax.

Dani reads the certificate until Alex gets between her arms and blocks the view with his head.

"That's you," he says.

"That's really nice, Alex," Dani says. She feels the gulf opening again and although she's nervous about having to tell Mrs. Alex, she's also relieved: *This is the last time! The last time I have to be in this house.*

"I picked the picture and Mrs. Alex changed the hair so it looks like you."

"I guess she likes it," says Mrs. Alex. "So what's up? We're about to head to my mom's. She's indulging her shopaholic tendencies. She wants to get him some beach stuff and I don't know what all else."

"Can you stay five minutes?" Dani asks. "I really need to talk to you, and it won't take longer than that. It's about our little guy here." She flaps her arm chicken-style to make her elbow dig into Alex's back, and he laughs. "Can we talk privately?"

"I'm sorry, Dani. I should have returned your calls. But I kept getting this feeling you were calling to quit, and that's the last thing I need to hear right now."

"I told Mom you weren't quitting," Alex says. "Because you like coming here, so you would never stop, right?"

"Can we talk privately?" Dani says again.

Mrs. Alex still refuses to sit down. She looks indignant. "I think Alex should have a say in who his babysitter is," she tells Dani.

I didn't prepare for Alex being here, Dani thinks.

"You! You!" Alex chants, pounding his fist on Dani's leg.

"This is for grown-ups, buddy," Dani tells Alex. She eases him to the floor, making his sneakers light up.

Alex turns around to look at her. "You're a grown-up?"

"Okay." Mrs. Alex sighs. "Let's set you up in your room with some cartoons. Grammy can wait."

"Will you still be here after my cartoons?" Alex asks.

"I don't think so," Dani tells him. She wants to ruffle his hair, not to check for blood but just because she likes him. But this is the day to stop touching him.

"Are you coming tomorrow?" he asks.

Mrs. Alex should rush up the stairs with him, but she doesn't. She stands there. "Well, answer him. Are you?"

"This is for grown-ups. Really. Shoosh upstairs and see your cartoons, little guy," Dani says. Does Mrs. Alex have to make it so hard?

"Oh no," Mrs. Alex says, scoping the messy room. She must be thinking about all the things that won't go right, that have teetered on going wrong, without Dani.

Alex starts upstairs, still looking at Dani. The lights on his sneakers flash between the vertical bars of the railing. Mrs. Alex starts up behind him, moving quietly in her slippers, not rushing in the stiff-legged way she does in her high heels.

"Is she quitting?" Alex whispers on the stairs.

Dani waits while Mrs. Alex settles Alex upstairs. She hears him crying, then becoming quiet when the cartoon starts. Mrs. Alex makes a phone call upstairs, probably to Alex's grammy.

"I do need to quit," Dani says when Mrs. Alex comes back and sits opposite her. Dani drops the certificate onto the coffee table.

"I was afraid so," Mrs. Alex replies, getting a set look to her face. It's the kind of look that says, *Why me? Why doesn't anything go right in my life?* She's probably numbering the two or three other nurses who quit the hospital and haven't been replaced, the boyfriend who came along after Tarzan Daddy and looked serious but went back to his ex-wife. Dani hates to put more on Mrs. Alex's plate. But leaving is the best for Alex and, ultimately, for everybody.

"I'm sorry, Cynthia," Dani says. "I'm just so sorry."

"What's wrong?" Mrs. Alex asks. "Somebody else is offering you more? Will you at least tell me how much they're offering so I can try to match it?"

"It's not that."

"Grammy and I discussed it and she said she'd help. We both agree you're the best possible sitter Alex could have. With Grammy contributing, and if I stretch a little, I can offer you—nine dollars an hour."

"It's not that." Dani squeezes her hands together. *I don't want to hurt anyone.* "Other stuff is going on in my life."

"Are you not getting your schoolwork done? You know, you don't have to spend every minute with Alex. I've talked to him. He knows you need homework time and you can't entertain him twenty-four-seven."

Dani shakes her head. "It's not that. School is fine. I mean, I might hand in a late assignment like everyone else, but school is normal."

"Then what is it? Tell me. Maybe we can work something out." She puts on a listening face. *This is going to be rough,* Dani thinks. *I didn't expect kindness and understanding.* It's clever of Mrs.

Alex, who is a tough, wily survivor of difficult situations.

"It's not practical stuff. It's something with me. An emotional thing I'm going through. I need to get away from here for a while."

Mrs. Alex tucks one leg under her. She seems eager for a chat, the way Beth had been. Dani imagines her sitting like that with her sorority in nursing school. Her crowd club-hopped around Boston with guys from the nearby pharmacology school. At least if Dani was going to wreck her schedule by talking, Mrs. Alex probably thought, it would be a fun talk. "I hope you know you can always talk to me about emotional stuff. I was seventeen once, you know. Is it that boy you've been telling me about? The singer?"

Dani had mentioned that Gordy called and invited her over, but she had told Mrs. Alex no more than that.

Dani pauses. In the pause Mrs. Alex seems cheerful but impatient. Her eyes drift upstairs, where the phone has started ringing. It must be Grammy, calling to find out what's taking so long. Alex's voice comes on in the recording.

Dani's eyes flick upstairs to make sure Alex is still in his room and not coming down the steps. She doesn't want him to overhear, ever; she never wants him to know. Dani wanted to be businesslike and impersonal and not reveal any bad stuff. Life is bad for her, but the badness shouldn't spread onto anyone else. There's no reason to alarm anyone if Dani can go away and deal with it on her own.

But Mrs. Alex isn't letting Dani go. Mrs. Alex isn't letting Dani handle it the way she thinks it should be handled. No matter what, this has to be the last time Dani comes here. What can

Dani do or say to make sure she isn't in this living room at this time tomorrow? There's only one way to protect Alex. The only way out is through the middle.

"Okay . . . ," she starts, and she's as nervous as she's ever been, that flying-up-out-of-your-body adrenaline fear that she and Shelley talked about, that occurs when you're summoned to the principal's office or have to speak in front of hundreds of people. She needs a suitable expression on her face. She's about to say something surprising and upsetting, and she needs to make it less scary. How can she put Mrs. Alex at ease? *Try smiling when you say it*, her mind tells her. *Maybe that will help. That's right,* she thinks. *I'll try smiling.* She hopes it isn't the nervous smile she had as a kid when her mom was angry or caught her in a lie, because then she'll seem like a complete psycho. She looks Mrs. Alex right in the face.

"I keep having these thoughts about killing Alex."

Mrs. Alex's head tilts to the side.

Her eyes widen.

part 3 THE OTHER SIDE

24

Oh no, Dani thinks. I never wanted to say *kill*.

Mrs. Alex sits with her head tilted and her chin pulled in.

"I guess I should go," Dani says, reaching for her backpack. Tonight could have gone better, but she's leaving this nightmare behind, and the only person who shared it was Mrs. Alex. More people could have been dragged into it—Shelley, Gordy, Beth, maybe even Alex—but they weren't. A contained nightmare of one night, with a beginning and end as crisp as a calendar.

"No," Mrs. Alex says. "Stay a minute. Sit right there." She glances up, hearing footsteps on the stairs. "I'll deal with Alex."

"All right," Dani says. She drops onto the couch, sitting à la Mrs. Alex with one foot beneath her. She had not predicted this calm reaction. She wonders if Mrs. Alex is about to go into adult mode, surrogate-mother mode, and offer a reasonable talk and some advice. Or will she—oh no, not again—ask her to stay on? Maybe, for the third time, offer more money?

Mrs. Alex shoos Alex back up the stairs, and Dani hears them talking in the hall. Mrs. Alex says, "Do you need to pee?" and Alex says, "I don't know," and Mrs. Alex says, "Let's go together." The bathroom door closes.

Ten minutes later, the doorbell rings. Mrs. Alex doesn't come down. Dani goes to the foot of the stairs.

"Do you want me to get it?" she calls up.

"If you don't mind," Mrs. Alex shouts from the bathroom.

Dani opens the door. Two policemen stand outside.

"Is Mrs. Draper present?" one asks.

"She's upstairs," Dani says. "She should be down in a minute."

"We'd like to speak with her. Is Alex here also?"

"He's up with his mom. Can I tell her who's . . . ?"

The police show their badges. "I'm Sergeant Mason of the Hawthorne Police," the older one says, "and this is Officer Pinto. What's your name, miss?"

"Dani Solomon."

"Would you come outside with me, Dani, so I can talk to you?"

"Sure." *So this is how it plays out,* she thinks as she realizes what's happening. In the arrest scenario she'd imagined so many times, Mrs. Alex and the police didn't act so normal, so calm and quiet. She had pictured screaming, blood, and sirens.

"I'll check on them upstairs," Officer Pinto says, going to the second floor where Alex's cartoons still play.

Dani steps outside onto the mat where she used to hesitate before ringing the bell.

"How old are you, Dani?" Sergeant Mason asks. He's tall and stocky with a gray goatee. His cruiser is parked in the Alexes' driveway.

"I'm seventeen."

"Do you know why we're here?"

"Because Mrs. Draper called you?"

So Dani is being arrested now. She doesn't have to panic

or even worry. She doesn't think of Mrs. Alex's phone call as a betrayal. The relief of having told Mrs. Alex overwhelms everything that's happening now or could happen in the future. Cause and effect, as she learned in school. Everything that occurs in the world is due to cause and effect.

Mason hands her a small yellow card, and he recites what the card says. "You have the right to remain silent. If you give up the right to remain silent, anything you say can and will be used against you in a court of law. You have the right to an attorney. If you desire an attorney and cannot afford one, an attorney will be obtained for you before police questioning."

"You can question me if you want to," Dani says.

"Do you know why Mrs. Draper may have called 911?"

"I told her I had thoughts about hurting Alex."

"That's her little boy?"

"Yes."

"That's a little unsettling, don't you think?"

"I know. I agree with you."

"You had thoughts about harming Alex?"

"Exactly." Dani stands up straight. She answers in a calm, even voice. She has always liked police officers, and she feels that they and she are on the same side. She wants them to know that she has no desire to obstruct the law.

"In what specific way would you harm Alex?" Sergeant Mason continues.

"Specifically, I would get one of the big knives from the kitchen and stab him while he was sleeping." Dani hopes that didn't sound sarcastic. Having never been interrogated before, she wants to answer the questions as completely as she can.

"That's unsettling," Sergeant Mason says again, reaching for his notebook.

"I don't really want to, though," Dani says quickly. "I'm actually glad Mrs. Draper called you, because I had been trying and trying to get out of babysitting, but I couldn't get her to take my calls."

"You don't want to hurt Alex? Then why did you tell Mrs. Draper that?"

"Because I kept thinking about it, and I figured she should know, just so Alex would be safe."

"Tell me exactly what happened when you threatened Alex. What did you say or do to him?"

"I never threatened Alex."

"Did you tell him you wanted to harm him?"

"No. Oh God, no." Dani squeezes her hands. She still has that up-in-the-air feeling.

"Did you tell Mrs. Draper you want to harm Alex?"

"I don't want to harm Alex. But I had these pictures in my mind. So I told Mrs. Alex I should leave. I didn't even want to come today. I wanted to quit. I did just quit babysitting and I wanted to leave, except that she told me to wait."

He closes his notebook, seeming to have decided something. "I see no intent to commit a crime here. I'm going to pop upstairs and tell Mrs. Draper. She seems pretty shaken up. Wait here. I want a few more words with you." He goes to the stairs, swinging his broad shoulders. He does a little skip on the bottom step that suggests to Dani her situation is not serious.

Almost over, she thinks. *A few more words and I'm free. A little awkwardness, that's all, and a promise to never see the Alexes again. I can handle that. I can find plenty of ways to fill my time.*

Sergeant Mason returns with his radio in hand. "Do you live with your parents?"

"With my mom."

"Beth Solomon, the real estate broker, right? How much does she know about this?"

"Nothing. I tried to tell her, but she didn't understand."

"Is she home right now?"

"She could be home. She's been painting the house."

"I think we should get you home and make sure she knows what's going on."

"May I go home alone and tell her?" Dani asks. "I think I would rather handle this myself."

He smiles without showing his teeth—a little sarcastic or smug, patronizing, as Gordy would say. "Why don't we give you a ride home to see if she's there? I'd like to talk with your mom and get this straightened out. Dot all the *i*'s."

"But I'm not arrested?"

"No. Unless there's something you haven't told me, you haven't committed any crime."

"So the siren won't be on or the lights flashing? That would freak my mom out."

"Nope. It'll look like we're giving you a ride home."

"All right, then. Can I get my pack from the living room?"

Dani sees no sign of Alex or Mrs. Alex, so she doesn't say good-bye. Good-bye forever. They seem as far inside as you can get, like the house is a chambered nautilus and they've spiraled to the innermost point. She wants to tell them both that she hopes they'll be able to find a good sitter. If Mrs. Alex had listened to her before, they might have found someone by now. Grammy will probably have to fill in for a while.

Dani walks to the cruiser. She's aware of cars slowing down to rubberneck. She wonders if Mrs. Alex has called friends or neighbors, and what she may have told them. Dani wonders about calling Beth to warn her what's about to happen.

She squeezes the handle of the passenger door but finds it locked.

Sergeant Mason is behind her. "Here you go, dear," he says, opening the door to the backseat. Dani laughs—of course she'll ride in back. She slides in. A Plexiglas window separates front seat from back, like in a taxi.

The passenger seat is for Officer Pinto, who climbs in next but doesn't look at her. He squints and shakes his head at Mason as they pull out. Maybe Mrs. Alex told him something terrible, something Mrs. Alex believed but wasn't true.

Dani taps the glass and Officer Pinto slides a panel open. The Plexiglas makes her feel like a perp, like they might be afraid of her. Pinto looks angry. Maybe they're doing that thing from the movies, where they take two roles. Good cop, bad cop.

"Are you going to tell my mother what I told Alex's mom?" she asks the friendly cop.

He speaks into the rearview mirror. "She should know what's going on, don't you think?"

Officer Pinto exhales through his lower teeth: *Sssss*. This makes Dani nervous. He must be Malcolm's father or uncle. They have the same last name and the same blue-black hair, except he has a bald spot she can see from the backseat. She hopes that all this will end without Malcolm finding out. She hopes there is a law that grants confidentiality to people who are just driven home and not arrested.

"Mom's going to be surprised," Dani says.

"I imagine so," Mason replies. "You say you didn't confide in her about any of this?"

"I tried to talk to her, but she didn't understand."

The cop shrugs. "Something tells me we're about to get her attention. Give me your address, dear."

Dani gives her address, and Sergeant Mason repeats it to someone—presumably headquarters—on the radio.

"Rich kid," Officer Pinto mutters.

They drive along the depot, where the afternoon train from Boston spills its briefcased commuters. The siren isn't on and the lights aren't flashing.

Officer Pinto slides the panel open. He speaks to Dani for the first time, without smiling.

"Is there anything else you need to tell us? Anything you may have said or done to that little boy? We have to call Social Services, you know. They'll question him, and anything that needs to come out is going to come out. It might be better if you tell us now."

"Nothing," Dani says. She pictures Alex being questioned by

a stiff-backed lady in a suit. She doubts he has anything damaging to say other than that she sometimes talked to Shelley on her cell phone when she was supposed to be playing with Louie. She doesn't want anyone to talk to Alex about her if they don't really have to, but she doesn't know how to stop them.

"Dear, answer me honestly," Sergeant Mason asks. "Is this stabbing business something you cooked up? Is it a cock-and-bull story you made up just to get out of babysitting?"

"No," Dani answers. "I didn't make it up. I didn't make up any of it."

"No further questions until we see the mother," Sergeant Mason tells his partner. "They might want to get somebody."

"Get somebody who?" Dani asks.

"Your mom may want to hire a lawyer. I would advise you not to tell me or Officer Pinto or anyone else any more about this, if you can help it. That's what that yellow card says."

They're a few blocks from school, and Dani sees three guys she knows walking with a basketball. She considers ducking, but that would make it look like she's done something wrong.

"Wait. Officer? Sir?" she asks the one driving.

"What's that, dear?"

"Can we not go past the high school? I don't want to see anybody I know. I mean, would they really believe you were only giving me a ride home?"

The policeman signals and turns left, avoiding the school by a couple of blocks.

"That's the kind of thing you're supposed to consider beforehand," Officer Pinto tells Dani.

25

Beth sees the cruiser in the driveway and opens the front door. The police officers follow Dani.

"Dani! What's wrong?"

"I'm okay, Mom." The odor of wet paint restores Dani. Like avocado-and-cucumber lotion, it's the smell of Beth and home. Dani feels the corners of her mouth sag, but she doesn't cry. She'll wait till the officers leave. Then she'll cry as much as she wants.

"What happened, Dani?" Beth turns to address the officers. "Was there an accident? Is she hurt?"

"I've been through a rough time, Mom," she says, "but now it's done and I'm just glad it's over."

"Oh my God, are you all right?" Beth scans Dani for signs of trouble—cuts, bruises, bandages, torn clothing. "What's going on? Did someone hurt Dani?"

"Your daughter's having some problems, ma'am. Why don't we go inside and talk about it?"

Beth lets them in. "What kind of problems is she having?"

"Apparently she indicated to the mother of the child she baby-sits for—," Officer Pinto begins.

Sergeant Mason stops him and nods at Dani. "Why don't you tell your mother yourself?"

"Mom, my mind has been feeling funny. I was having all these thoughts I didn't really want to have." Dani's voice sounds childish, even to her. She didn't realize how relieved she would feel to be home with Beth.

"Your mind? Oh, Dani, what's wrong? Are you depressed? Do you need to see a doctor?" Beth gets between Dani and the police and wraps her arms around her.

"Just a moment, ma'am," Officer Pinto says. "Young lady, why don't you tell your mother exactly why we made a call at Mrs. Draper's house?"

"All right, Mike," says the older cop. "Why don't I do this?" The younger partner wiggles his head as if he's bored. Dani gets the floating-up feeling she had when she told Mrs. Alex. Things would have been so different two days ago if she had been able to tell her mother at the time and in the way she had wanted to. Now her mother is asking what's wrong, the bad cop is making her tell what's wrong, and what's wrong is known by too many people. She feels the wrongness seeping from the other side of the line into this life.

"It's so awful, Mom. I can barely tell you." That childish wailing again. She grabs Beth's hand.

"It's okay. Tell me."

"I keep thinking about hurting Alex."

Dani expected Beth's face to come closer. But her expression turns inward, the way Mrs. Draper's had. Maybe she's seeing pictures like the ones Dani saw.

"Is Alex okay? Did you hurt him? Is that why they brought you here? Is Alex . . . dead?"

"Alex is alive, Mom. I didn't hurt him." Beth isn't connecting this conversation to the one Dani tried to have.

"Does your daughter have a history of mental illness, ma'am?" Officer Pinto asks.

"Alex isn't hurt? No one's hurt?"

"No, they're not hurt. Ma'am, does your daughter have a history of mental illness? Ever threaten to hurt or kill anyone in the family? Anyone at school?"

"Kill anyone at school? Oh my God. What kind of question is that?" She stares from one officer to the other.

"I didn't do anything, Mom," Dani wails. She's crumbling and she needs all of her mother's attention. "I just kept thinking about it."

"But why? Why would you want to hurt Alex? I thought you loved Alex!"

"I never wanted to hurt Alex. I kept asking to get out of babysitting, but Mrs. Alex wouldn't let me go. I'm just glad it's over."

Dani wants *over* to be the word everyone hears.

"I can't believe you or anyone would think about hurting little Alex," Beth says. She turns to the police. "Did she do anything? Has she done anything? Tell me she hasn't done anything."

"You don't have to tell us right now," Sergeant Mason answers, "but someone is going to ask whether there is a history of this nature." When he puts his hands on his hips he looks broad enough to protect someone. "I suggest—and I cannot stress this strongly enough—that you make an appointment with a psychologist. You may also want to retain a lawyer, in case news of this gets out, or in case Mrs. Draper pursues any legal action."

"What kind of legal action would it be?" Beth Solomon asks, envisioning something, starting to shift ahead. Maybe there are events to come from this, bad events, that Dani hasn't thought of yet. She's still looking forward to the relief part.

"You never threatened that child, correct?" Mason asks in a kind voice.

"I told you, no. It's still no. Can you leave me now so I can rest? Can I be alone with my mother?"

"You're probably all right, then," he says to Beth. He even winks at her, but Beth doesn't notice.

The younger officer speaks. "Do you monitor her online activities, ma'am? Has she ever sent death threats over the Internet?"

"That's enough, Mike," Mason says. "Did Mrs. Draper say anything about death threats on the Internet?"

"She did not, but I regard it as a routine line of questioning."

"Dani, have you?" Beth was starting to sit, but she gets up again. She looks drained, like her skin has gotten too big for her body.

"Of course not!" Dani says. "You know I would never do that, Mom."

"I wouldn't respond to any of this, ma'am," Mason suggests. "Not until you see a lawyer."

"I wonder just what it is you know and don't know," Pinto persists. "Did you have any inkling of this, ma'am?"

"No . . ." It took a while, but Beth is crumbling too. When the cops came in she was ready to protect Dani. Now Beth blinks a few times and looks from Mason to Pinto to Dani, with dampness trapped in her eyelashes. "I didn't know about it. How long has this been going on, Dani?"

Dani plops down on the couch. "A few weeks."

"A few weeks? It's been going on a few weeks." Beth consults some internal calendar and closes her eyes.

"Ma'am," Sergeant Mason begins, "I'm a parent too. And if my kid ever said something like this, I would find it unsettling. I would not delay in taking her to a psychologist or therapist."

"All right," Beth says. "You hear that, honey? We'll find a therapist. I'll start calling around tomorrow." Mason leans toward her. "Today," Beth says.

Dani knows Beth is thinking about all she needs to do today, meetings and client appointments and searches in the registry of deeds, to which the therapist calls will have to be added.

"Did you have to park a cruiser in front of my house?" Beth asks.

Sergeant Mason smiles. "That's the car I work in, ma'am."

"I don't think Dani's done anything wrong."

"Let's hope not."

"I think it's the stress," Beth says, pressing her hands to the bridge of her nose, "with school and tennis and music and college applications and so on. And I wasn't home often enough."

"Lots of kids are under stress these days, ma'am," Mason says.

"I don't think she did anything wrong. Yet you've parked a marked police car in front of my house. Was there any reason to bring her here? Couldn't you have called from the station?"

Dani looks out at the driveway. The elderly couple across the street methodically removes bags of groceries from the trunk. The woman passes them to the man, who carries them inside. Neither of them seems to notice the squad car. They're sweet elderly people, but Dani stopped waving to them when she started having thoughts about yelling that they would die soon.

The cops exchange looks. "She's your child," Mason says. "She's living at this address, and she should be home."

Beth moves closer to the door. "What will I say when people ask why a cruiser was parked in front of my house?"

Pinto smirks. "Tell them you got a visit from the parenting police."

"I didn't know anything about this until you walked in the door five minutes ago."

"You should pay more attention to your kids, ma'am," Pinto pushes.

"Kid, singular," Beth says.

"Tell me, ma'am," Pinto asks, "where is your husband?"

Beth smirks. "I killed him. Joke!"

"We have another call," Mason says.

"Just one more question," Beth says. "Is this going to be in the papers?"

"It's up to me if I want it in the police log. I've suggested you take your daughter to see somebody. I'll check back in a week to see if you've done that."

"All right," Beth says. "But call next time. Don't just . . . drive up like that."

"Good luck, ma'am," says Pinto.

Mason claps Dani's shoulder. "No more trouble from you, okay, young lady?"

Dani has a lot of experience smiling under stress. That's from both winning and losing tennis matches. "Thank you for bringing me home," she tells them.

"She seems like a nice girl," Mason tells Beth.

Because Beth has been painting, the windows are open. Dani hears Officer Pinto on his way to the car.

"Nice girl? She's a freaking whack job," he says to Mason. "And it's always the rich parents who have their heads in the sand."

26

"Oh, thank God it's over. I wanted to tell you, but I didn't know how to say it. Can you see why I had trouble making people understand, because it's so weird? But now I told and babysitting is finally over."

Dani kept it together when the police were in the house. Now she feels like throwing up tears. She's taller than her mother, but she needs the sensation of someone solid and established taking charge of her situation. She inhales the smells of her mother's lotion and paint and fabric softener.

Beth hugs Dani. "It's all right. It's all right," she says into Dani's hair. "Dani, did you tell me everything? Did you hurt Alex?"

"Mom, of course not!"

"Is there anything you didn't tell the police? Did you ever touch Alex . . . sexually? If there is anything at all, this isn't the time to keep secrets. You have to tell me now so we can get a lawyer."

"Alex? No. That's so gross." The grossness of it propels Dani into walking away, the same way Shelley helplessly waved her hands while thinking about touching Mr. Gabler.

"Then what did you do?"

"I never did anything. I kept picturing weird things happening, and I didn't want them to happen, so I told Mrs. Alex I couldn't babysit anymore. That's all."

"What kind of weird things?"

"Like stabbing him or something."

Beth follows Dani to the far corner of the room. "I wish I could see inside your mind. You look the same as you did yesterday. But the things I hear you saying . . . We have to get a doctor."

"Okay, we'll get a doctor."

"So what did you tell Mrs. Alex? How much does she know?"

"That I had thoughts of harming Alex."

"Why did you tell her that?"

"So she could get another babysitter. Are you going to call a doctor now?"

"What did Mrs. Alex say when you told her?"

"She didn't say much. She immediately called the cops."

"You shouldn't have told Mrs. Alex anything. You should have just quit."

"I tried. She wouldn't let me."

"If something like this ever happens again—"

Dani sits on the couch. "I'm never babysitting again. It isn't going to happen."

"Oh, Dani." Beth scoots over to Dani and pulls Dani's head onto her shoulder. Dani can tell her mom is trying to figure out how to tell Sean. This will be one of only three times in Dani's life that her mother hasn't been proud of her. The other two were when Dani made her mother a Valentine's Day card from a nonexistent secret admirer, and the time Dani was late for the concert. "It should have been you and me having that conversation, not you and Mrs. Alex."

"I tried two days ago, I said."

"That was your way of telling me? You could have said it was an emergency."

"Oh, well." Dani wraps her arms around herself.

Beth presses her hands to her face again. The right hand wears a ring from Sean that he called a friendship ring. Beth spent hours on the phone with her friends discussing the ring's significance, whether it meant she was pre-engaged. One friend said, "I didn't know people used the term 'friendship ring' anymore."

"Dani, why do you think you're doing this?"

"It doesn't feel like something I'm doing. It feels like something that's happening to me. I think Sergeant Mason is right. I think I'd like to talk to somebody."

"Dani, is somebody putting ideas like this into your head?"

"No."

"Who are you spending time with these days? Is it still Shelley, or are you with a different crowd? I feel like I've been ignoring you lately and I know that isn't good."

"It's still Shelley."

"I should start calling around. We need a really good therapist. Not just any hippie-dippie who can hang up a shingle."

"Mom, would you sit with me a few minutes? Then we'll make the appointment? And then can we go to the movies and the sandwich place? I think a good movie might rinse some of the bad stuff out of my mind."

Beth strokes Dani's hair. "I need to catch my breath a minute, honey. This is a lot to hit me with."

It's over, Dani tells herself. Finally she doesn't have to go back and babysit. Finally she doesn't have to be alone with Alex. Her problem with the bad thoughts had seemed to be expanding, picking up power and momentum and spreading into every area of her life. But she did the right thing and told Alex's mom. That's the bottom line. Her shame and embarrassment meant nothing in comparison to Alex's need to be safe. It was awkward and horrifying to have to discuss the thoughts with the police and Beth. It was absolute hell to discuss it with Mrs. Alex. But Dani has put Alex first, and so she privately congratulates herself with the same word she used for Shelley. *I'm brave,* she thinks. *I may be crazy, but I'm brave.*

But her relief lasts only for moments, because an old saying starts to run through her mind like a musical loop: Where there's a will, there's a way. The fact that she's no longer babysitting doesn't mean that she won't kill Alex. A new thought comes into her mind, of going to Alex's house and dragging him home to her house and murdering him there.

Not after all that work, Dani thinks. *Not after all I've done. Finding someone to listen to me. Asking and asking. Telling and telling. Involving the police and Mom and Mrs. Alex and everyone. I thought it was over. I tried to end it. How can I still have these thoughts?* She thought she had left them behind, but they followed her here. The thoughts are like the water that comes into a hole you dig in the sand, Dani realizes. If you create an empty space, they will fill it. She looks at her hands and squeezes them together. *I'm not hurting anyone; I haven't hurt anyone; at least as of this exact minute, I still have not hurt anyone.*

Beth puts her hands on top of Dani's. "Tough day, huh?" She's trying to understand.

"Will you start calling the doctors now?" Dani asks. "I think it'll be a big relief to talk to someone."

"I'll start calling around, but no movie tonight. You look done in and so am I. Once I make some calls we'll pop some supper in the microwave and go to bed early."

"Would you do me a favor, Mom?" Dani asks.

"Of course, sweetheart."

"Will you lock your door when you go to bed?"

Beth takes a few seconds to realize what Dani's saying. When she does, it seems that Beth might find this worse than the thoughts of hurting Alex. She puts her hands over her eyes and takes a deep breath.

"You think about hurting me, too? Why would you want to hurt me?"

Dani stands in front of Beth with her hands folded.

"Would you just do it, Mom? It would make me feel better."

"Well, am I . . . safe?"

"I'm tired and I need to sleep somewhere," Dani says. "That's all I can tell you. Now will you do it?"

After their supper, Dani hears Beth lock her bedroom door. She locks it so softly it seems she doesn't want Dani to hear. Beth might think it's mean and insulting, but it makes Dani feel better. Dani wishes she could feel closer to her mom right now. Dani feels like the one person in the world who wants to help her—and who *can* help her—is a locked door away. But she had to ask Beth for that favor. If everyone is protected from Dani, she feels safer too.

27

"It's fine," Beth Solomon tells her neighbor Lynette the next day, when Lynette asks about the cruiser. Lynette is someone Beth usually can talk to about anything. "Dani got stranded at school and ended up talking with the cop who patrols the school. He saw her standing there and offered her a ride home. Apparently she tried to call me, but I was talking to a client and didn't check my messages. No reason to worry."

28

Text messages between Shelley and Dani:

"You haven't told anyone, have you? You're still the only one who knows."

"Of course not. You are my best friend and I will never tell anyone your secret."

29

"I guess I just like being around her," Shelley says. "It's not that I need to have this kind of relationship or that kind. I mean, she doesn't need to know that my feelings for her are different than for any other friend. I just want to spend time getting to know her. I just want her in my life."

Shelley and Dani are hunkered on their bench, constructing what they know of Meghan's relationship history. Meghan seems to like getting boys from Hawthorne High interested, but she only dates them two or three times before dropping them.

"She's not the kind of person who gets her whole identity from being part of a couple," Shelley says. "I think that's cool."

"I agree," says Dani. She and Shelley are not those kinds of people either.

Dani has already decided not to tell Shelley what happened with Mrs. Alex and the police. It's over and done with, and anyway, judging from their earlier conversation, Shelley may not be much help. Dani still has thoughts about grabbing Mr. Gabler's testicles. But no way is she mentioning that to Shelley again.

30

Dani goes for her first visit with Dr. Kumar, whose office has silk throw pillows from India and a painting of a bowl of cherries.

"Are you angry at someone, Daniela?" Dr. Kumar asks. "Are you angry at Alex for any reason? Are you angry at Mrs. Alex?"

Dani tells Dr. Kumar about Mrs. Alex staying out late, being disorganized, and not having food in the house, but no, she doesn't think she's angry at either Alex or Mrs. Alex.

"Do you have thoughts about harming anyone else?"

Dani tells Dr. Kumar her thoughts of knocking her mother off a ladder, grabbing Mr. Gabler's testicles, and outing Shelley in front of the opposing team, and about Gordy in a basement with pieces beside other pieces they should never be beside. But she doesn't feel angry at those people. She gets irritated at her mother and Shelley sometimes. But not angry enough to do those things.

"And your relationship with your father, Daniela? Would you describe it as an angry relationship?"

Dr. Kumar has beautiful, heavily made-up eyes, a blond streak in her hair, and white boots that make her look like a superhero. Her outfit the first day is an amethyst-colored dress with multiple silver necklaces.

Dani tells Dr. Kumar what Dr. Kumar has already heard from Beth: that Rob Solomon moved out when Dani was eight to live with another woman and her three children and they all moved to Colorado together. Dani visited a few times and did outdoor things with her dad, but she didn't feel like she belonged there. For a while she was sad, but now all that seems like a long time ago. Beth was angry about Colorado, very angry, but she seemed to accept it once she met Sean.

"Are you experiencing stress at school? Are you going through a stressful period?"

She tells Dr. Kumar about the tough competitors she and Shelley may face in this year's MIAA semifinals. About applying to her mother's alma mater, a great school, but also a couple of safety schools. About rehearsing with Gordy once a week, and how Shelley had a movie date with someone she likes who, Shelley just told Dani, touched her for no reason twenty to twenty-five times during the course of the movie.

It's good having Dr. Kumar to talk to, so Dani schedules three more appointments. She thinks she'll enjoy coming back here and looking at beautiful things, including Dr. Kumar herself and her jewel-toned wardrobe. Being here has another advantage. Dani didn't want to hurt Alex, but she was never a hundred percent sure that she wouldn't hurt him. If anything ever does happen, by telling several people she's spread the responsibility around. Mrs. Alex, Sergeant Mason, Officer Pinto, Beth, and now Dr. Kumar, even if they are shocked by her thoughts, are like legs that give her stability. Each of them, by knowing, is taking on a bit of the weight. As days go by and she doesn't have to babysit, Dani hopes her strange other-side life with Alex might chip off like a chunk of ice that breaks off in a thawing river and spirals away, never to be seen again.

31

"Well?" Beth Solomon asks in the car on the way home from Dani's appointment. Beth looks hopeful, like a little kid you would hate to disappoint.

"We talked a lot," Dani answers. "I liked her."

"I knew you would," Beth says, looking satisfied. "Do you feel a little better?"

"Definitely. I made the same appointment for the next three weeks."

"That's great," Beth says. She adds the appointments to her phone and then pulls into traffic. "Whatever this is, it didn't flare up in a day, and it won't take just a day to get rid of it either."

32

At their second rehearsal, Dani and Gordy watch Sonny and Cher sing "I Got You, Babe."

"My dad loves this," he says. "He and my mom used to sing it to each other."

When the video ends, Dani and Gordy sing the song together. She does the harmony differently from the recording. They look into each other's eyes and swing their upper bodies from side to side as if they have long cascades of hair like Cher's. The way Gordy does this doesn't seem like a drag queen. It seems simultaneously feminine, respectful, and athletic.

When they're done, Gordy goes to the kitchen and comes back with two pints of premium ice cream, one of banana and one of Heath bar. Dani remembers the horror of Icey's and Meghan. What a difference two weeks can make. They sit on the couch with their feet up and start eating one pint each, then trade. This is a time when Dani would normally have been babysitting.

"I'm free!" she says, waving her spoon in the air.

"How come you stopped?" Gordy asks. "They didn't need you anymore?"

"It was getting to be too much," Dani says. She shivers and shakes her head, mouths the word *ugh* without actually saying it.

She's thinking about the bad times, but maybe Gordy will think she just has an ice cream headache.

"Too bad. You seemed to really like that little kid."

"I did. I started missing him on day one." She considers telling Gordy about the time Alex used all his game points to buy Louie a Jacuzzi and then it turned out he didn't know what a Jacuzzi was. But although little kids say and do funny things, when you repeat them or act them out they don't seem as funny.

She wishes Gordy hadn't mentioned Alex. Because she's picturing Alex's body in the Alexes' driveway after someone, it must have been Dani, backed the car over him. What does a little kid's body look like after it's been run over? A short red streak, with cloth mixed in. She decides to have Gordy drive her past Alex's house on the way home so she can check the driveway.

Once she's decided to do that, Dani can focus on how ridiculously good-looking Gordy is. When the ice cream is gone they kiss for half an hour and they both taste like candy and banana.

33

Shelley eats her last chicken nugget with ranch dip. "So what do you think is with all the touching?" she asks.

Dani doesn't want to point out that Meghan is a craven attention hound. "Some people are more touchy-feely than others," she says.

"Maybe I'll see if she wants to hang out next weekend. I mean, if you and I aren't doing anything."

"Why don't you leave the ball in her court and see if she initiates something?" Dani's worried that Meghan, with her clear case of attention hound–ism, wants to be the pursued instead of the pursuer, and that all the risk will be on Shelley's side.

Dani stretches on the bench with her arms under her head. She knows Malcolm Pinto is staring—so what else is new?—but she's just trying to get comfortable.

"Be careful with Meghan, okay?" Dani says. "I think she likes having people infatuated with her."

"She does have them," Shelley says. "And you can see why."

"Mmm."

"You know," Shelley continues, "there are straight people around, weird straight people, who like to lead somebody on and then say, 'Oh my God, how could you think I would be interested in you when I'm straight?'"

"That's their little game, I guess," Dani says. "It sounds like an ego thing." She thinks, *Are you actually admitting that Meghan might have a flaw?*

"It happens pretty often, apparently." Shelley sips contemplatively from her energy drink. "You know, I've been going to GSA since September and I hear people's stories and I'm like, 'Yeah that's sad,' and I look so sympathetic, and I blend in as a straight person who's supporting the gay people. No one there knows about me. I'm starting to feel like a fake, as if all the other people have the courage to live their lives a certain way and I don't."

"Maybe what you're describing is true of lots of people in GSA. Maybe that's why the group is set up that way. So people who are . . ."

"Questioning."

". . . can see what goes on and how it all fits. But they don't have to disclose anything about themselves. Like, what happened at your first meeting? Did they go around the room and have everyone announce whether they were straight or gay?"

"Of course not. Because then I would know about Meghan."

"Meghan's in GSA? I didn't realize that."

"She joined after I did. Like, January."

"Not that that tells us anything."

"No, it doesn't. Hey, you probably wonder why I haven't asked you how it's going with Gordon."

"I figured my turn would come sooner or later." She playfully slaps Shelley as if Shelley has been rude.

"I haven't asked because it's so obvious. I can tell by looking at you how it's going."

"Swimmingly."

"I know you pretty well, I guess," Shelley says.

"Yes you do, my oldest and bestest friend."

34

That afternoon, Officers Pinto and Lomba see Dani and Shelley walking home from school.

"It's too bad about that girl there," Officer Pinto tells this afternoon's partner.

"The cute, sturdy one?"

"No, the one in the sweatshirt. That one—she just saw the cruiser and turned her head away. She looks like a nice girl, but she's a little sick."

35

"This house is getting too small," Mrs. Pinto says. "It felt fine a year ago, but since Micaela was born we feel crammed in." She speaks to her friend Mrs. Sokol on a small porch off the kitchen.

"The third child makes a difference," Mrs. Sokol agrees. She's here to pick up her son Kyle, who spent the afternoon with Malcolm.

"I guess it's time to look around for something bigger."

"This time, hold out for a larger driveway and a laundry room. Who do you think you'll use? I really liked Beth Solomon. She was incredibly patient when John decided to be a pain and kept canceling all our appointments. You might want to see if she's still selling houses. What? Why are you looking at me like that?"

"She's another one with her head in the sand," Mrs. Pinto says.

"What do you mean?"

"Apparently her daughter is severely troubled," Mrs. Pinto continues in a low voice. "I'm surprised Beth lets her out of the house every morning."

"Daniela? Why? What's wrong with her?" Mrs. Sokol has heard only positive things about Daniela, who was in Kyle's class for a few years. A lot of the kids in town have problems. Some of them grow up in Maple Ledge, a project run by the Hawthorne

Housing Authority that got the nickname Sharp Corners because the playground is littered with broken glass. Others come from families where the parents are abusing coke and even heroin. Some parents who seemed perfectly nice at parties keep their kids home on Mondays to hide the kids' black eyes. Dani always seemed like one of the good kids with good parents.

"The boys are still upstairs, right?" Mrs. Pinto whispers. "I don't want them to hear."

"The music is blasting up there. From the sound of it, they're playing Guitar Hero."

"Apparently Daniela was talking about killing a little kid she was babysitting for. Mike said they were unable to make an arrest, but only because of a technicality."

"You mean she was—what, holding him out the window, like Michael Jackson?"

"It's not funny, Carolyn."

"I know. But what did she actually do?"

"Apparently she talked about putting a knife to his throat. I shouldn't say any more. Mike talks when he's upset—you know some of the awful stuff they see and the sick, messed-up people they sometimes have to deal with—but he always swears me to secrecy."

"Whose kid was it?"

"You know I can't tell you anything like that."

"Oh, come on. You know I won't say anything."

"That's the one thing I absolutely cannot tell you."

"Oh my God, the kid's parents must be freaking out."

"Apparently she was going on about this knife idea to the mother of the child in a very casual tone, like it was the most normal thing in the world. And there's more."

"What?"

"Mike said the mother said that when Dani talked about it, she was smiling."

Malcolm Pinto slips across the kitchen floor in his socks. He opens the fridge. The bottom shelf used to be full of beer for his father, but now it's loaded with iced tea and soda. He takes two cans, one for himself and one for Kyle, and slips back to his room.

36

Malcolm closes the door to his room after Kyle has left.

Apparently Beth's daughter is severely troubled. Apparently Daniela was getting ready to kill a little kid she was babysitting for. Apparently she talked about putting a knife to his throat. Apparently she was going on about this knife idea to the mother of the child in a very casual tone, like it was the most normal thing in the world.

Dani again.

Dani Solomon is so not what she appears to be.

Apparently.

37

"So," Malcolm says as their truck idles in line for the town composting center. This time Mike let him drive. *So* is a funny word, Malcolm thinks. It's supposed to connect one part of a story to another. But you use it when you want to change the subject and are not sure how. "So, Dad . . . I heard something I wasn't supposed to hear."

"With regard to . . . ?" Mike asks.

"Your work stuff. Stuff that's happening in town."

"Who did you hear it from?"

"Mom was talking to Kyle's mom. She didn't think I was around." Malcolm inches the car forward.

"Your mother is a wonderful woman," Michael says, watching birds move in the treetops. "But she needs to know when to keep her mouth shut."

"She didn't know."

"So, what did you overhear?"

"About Dani. The little kid and the knife and the mother."

"Ah," Michael says. He sucks on his lower lip and nods. "Strawberry Nutcake."

"Did that really happen? It sounds unbelievable. I mean, it wasn't a joke or anything?"

Michael waves to show Malcolm the cars are moving.

"I'm not supposed to tell you what happens on the job. You know that."

"Okay. I'm just wondering if what Mom repeated is true. But I guess it is."

"I don't know how much your mother repeated. And I can neither confirm nor deny."

"Why would such a nice-seeming girl say and do things like that?" Malcolm asks. He's always liked these conversations with his dad, but this one feels different and important. He's not friends with Dani and Shelley—he doesn't even speak to them—but he always felt they were special, that they lived on a more refined level than most people. While he wants to know more about the knives, a younger part of him hopes it isn't true. Finding out for sure what his father knows is breaking his heart a little bit. At the same time, it will make him stronger. He'll be one of the people who know the score, who know the worst. The people in the driver's seat.

"Because," Michael says in a teacherly voice, "she seemed to be a sheep, but on closer inspection she is not a sheep."

"She's a wolf in sheep's clothing," Malcolm says. His father waves him forward. They're tenth in line, and the compost center is in sight.

"Aroooo!" Michael calls, imitating a wolf's howl. He slaps Malcolm on the arm.

"Aroooo!" Malcolm echoes.

38

"When is Dani coming to babysit?" Alex asks.

"Dani's gone," his mother says. "She moved away."

39

Cecilia Martin, English teacher, hands wineglasses to the women in her book group. They probably won't get around to discussing this month's pick, *The Heart Is a Lonely Hunter* by Carson McCullers. Tonight it's more important that they hear a real story—Cynthia Draper's story.

"I can't believe you feel up to book group after what you've been through," Cecilia told Cynthia on the phone two days earlier.

"How could I not come?" said Cynthia. "I need to talk about it. I feel more comfortable discussing it in a friend's home than anywhere else."

Cecilia's eyes narrow as Cynthia tells her story. She feels how Cynthia must have felt, confronted out of nowhere with a danger to Alex and having to use her wits to save him.

"Good call locking yourself in the bathroom," Cecilia says. Her wineglass makes a ring on Carson McCullers's face. "I don't think I would have had your presence of mind. I would have wigged out."

Kathleen Perkins recrosses her legs. "I would have taken her down right there. As they say in the Marines, kill 'em all and let God sort 'em out."

"She still shows up for school every day," Cecilia says. "That's the thing that gets me. I had her in English class today, and I kept wondering what goes on behind that innocent-looking face. I asked the school psychologist if she had been in—usually he's pretty open about that stuff—and he said no. At least now that I said something he'll know what her deal is, in case—in case I don't know what."

"Oh, she's supposedly getting help," Cynthia says. "Beth Solomon called right away to tell me that. She was obviously trying to do damage control."

"Woosh," Kathleen says. "That must have been quite a conversation."

"It wasn't," says Cynthia. "She made a point of leaving a message when she knew I would be at work. Obviously she wasn't eager to speak to me."

"I wonder if Dani is looking for another babysitting job," the teacher muses.

"No, no, no," Cynthia says. "We cannot let that happen."

"And you say she was smiling while she told you all this?" Kathleen asks.

"That's right," says Cynthia.

"Mmmmm-mm," Kathleen hums, imitating the creepy music in a horror movie.

"Do not let her babysit for you," Cynthia says. She clutches her wine and stares at the floor. The other women stare too, as if the portrait of a murdered child is worked into the carpet.

40

"Mom," Dani says. She carries her laptop into her mother's home office. "Mom. Would you look at this for a minute?"

She had gone to the Hawthorne *Beacon-Times* website to read the school sports page when she found this:

> Thursday, May 13
>
> SITTER TO MOM: I MIGHT KILL TOT
>
> A babysitter responsible for a five-year-old Hawthorne boy told the child's mother she contemplated killing him, the *Beacon-Times* learned on Tuesday.
>
> Sources close to the situation told the *Beacon-Times* that the sitter told police that she "kept thinking about" murdering the boy and "had a picture in her mind" of him dying. Sergeant Philip Mason of the Hawthorne Police Department confirmed the incident but told a reporter that no charges were filed and asked the *Beacon-Times* to keep the babysitter's name private.
>
> A source close to the situation said the sitter, a seventeen-year-old student at Hawthorne High School, revealed her intentions to the child's mother, who then called 911 and locked herself and the child in an upstairs bathroom while awaiting the arrival

of police. The *Beacon-Times* is withholding the name of the child's mother in order to protect the privacy of the potential victim. Police arriving on the scene found the sitter alone downstairs. According to Sergeant Mason, after questioning the teen, police returned her to the custody of her parents and urged a psychiatric evaluation, which subsequently took place. Sources did not reveal where the evaluation took place or what results were found.

Neighbors of the endangered child, interviewed by the *Beacon-Times* near the home where the incident occurred, were "stunned" to learn of the babysitter's intentions.

"Who could consider killing an innocent child?" asked one couple who lives near the family, when informed of the incident.

Beth reads the screen over Dani's shoulder. "My God," she says, "this wasn't supposed to happen. He said no newspapers."

"Nothing happened," Dani says. "Why would anyone even care?" Dani says. She and Beth scan the article again.

"My name isn't in it," Dani said. "My name isn't anywhere."

"Neither is mine," says Beth.

"Will people figure out that it's me?"

"It looks like Sergeant Mason kept his word," says Beth. "It must have been that other one."

"I could tell he didn't like me," Dani says.

"The little prick," says Beth. "This was supposed to be a private matter."

"Can anyone tell it's me?" Dani says. She's so surprised by the article that she can't trust herself to read it the way a classmate would.

"How many people know that you have a babysitting job?"

"A lot. I'm always having to miss stuff because of it. Or I used to."

"How many kids babysit?"

"Maybe thirty of the girls. And one or two of the boys. Usually it's their little brothers or sisters. I don't know if they get paid."

"No one can know it's you. It doesn't say our names, or Alex's name or Mrs. Alex's name or a street or even a neighborhood." Beth slaps the screen with the back of her hand. "'Contemplated killing him.' 'Endangered child.' I called Sergeant Mason and told him you had started with Dr. Kumar. He was nice about it, very encouraging. He thanked me for following up and said he hoped we were on the right track.

"It's that other one. Parenting police. The little bastard." Beth almost trips getting up from her desk. "Mason was right. We need a lawyer. I shouldn't have waited one minute before calling somebody."

"I'm sorry, Mom," Dani says. "I'm sorry this is getting expensive." Now they will hire a lawyer to keep her name out of the paper, and that will be the end of it.

"Why did you have to go and tell anyone else? Why didn't you just keep it between us?"

Dani knows she can say "I tried to tell you." But her mother is upset and it's all Dani's fault and she doesn't want to make it worse.

Beth grabs her phone and starts scrolling through names. "We need someone really, really good. I should give Donald Abt a call."

Dani covers the phone. "Don't call him, Mom, please. Please call someone else."

"Why?"

"Mom, I don't think he even does murder. He represents rock stars. He's an entertainment lawyer."

"But he'll know who to get. The best always know the best. I wouldn't know who to get. I know tax people and real estate people. Donald would know everyone in Boston. Once the word 'murder' has been mentioned, you need a Boston lawyer."

"Because I'm sort of seeing his son, Gordon. That's why. Now will you not call?"

"You're dating Donald Abt's son? Why didn't you tell me?"

"It was brand new. I didn't want to jinx it. I didn't want to make it a bigger deal than it was."

"How long has this been going on?"

"Please don't call his dad, Mom. Pick someone else. I'm begging you."

"Dani, we are in this now and we are not getting out of it any other way. If you're in this kind of trouble, who you're dating or not dating goes right out the window. We need the right representation before things get worse and you get carted off in handcuffs. And yes, it is expensive, and yes, it's a lot of trouble, but frankly I'm your parent and I'm responsible for everything you say and do and we can't let this go any further. And I still don't know why you would say something like that to Alex's mom."

"Mom, don't call Gordon's father. It's so humiliating. I'm just hoping he didn't see this. I hope he doesn't know it's me. Don't call. I'm begging you." She had tried to tell Gordon herself, or at least to hint, but his finding out by other means would be all wrong. She would look like someone with something to hide. That day on Shark's Jaw he had believed she was excellent, like him. And she had felt excellent that day too.

Beth pauses. "Okay, I'll call someone else. I'm sorry about your little romance, but you're not exactly in a position to call the shots right now. Here's what we're going to do: I won't call Donald Abt this minute, but if I don't make the connection I need to make in one hour, I'm calling him. And do me a favor today, okay, Dani? Don't call anyone, don't talk to anyone, don't e-mail anyone, don't text anyone, and definitely don't leave the house. Have you got that? No communication with anyone today."

Dani is reading the screen again, because there's more.

"Look at me, Dani. Have you got that? No e-mail."

"Got it. I'm really sorry, Mom. God, I hope no one figures out it's me.

"No names, no names," she chants as she scrolls down the page.

> Comments:
>
> Coastal160 wrote:
>
> Another impeccable job from Our Lokel Noospaper.
>
> It's just like them to get everything but the name.

fishies7 wrote:
Yeah, I'm surprised we didn't get her bra size. But not her name.

sick-of-it-all wrote:
Child-killers top my list of people who should be removed from society ASAP. I say fry 'em. No judge or courtroom needed. I'd be glad to throw the switch myself.

Coastal160 wrote:
What do you need—just a big ole chair with a couple strong straps and some juice?

Sanddollar wrote:
I know the mother of the kid this happened to, and she is in shock. Just shows that you don't know anything about people really.

peewe wrote:
The girl is obviously a severe nutcase. Everyone in Hawthorne is a bunch of drugged-up losers and now come to find out psychos too, no surprise there

Rowdie wrote:
The cops returned her home.

Waster wrote:
What a bunch of screw-ups.

Rowdie wrote:
They completely fell down on the job. This is probably not even going on the girl's permanent record. I'll be surprised if she doesn't end up with a job at a day care a few years from now. You can't trust the government to protect you. Some of us need to take matters into our own hands.

Coastal160 wrote:
Show up with torches and pitchforks. A real vigilante group just like the good old days.

Sheepdogg wrote:
I know who it is. When you find out you won't believe it.

Rowdie wrote:
Who is it then?

Sheepdogg wrote:
I can't tell you.

Dani's phone rings. She has a text message from Shelley: "Unreal! Who else do we know who babysits?"

"Phone," Beth says, extending her hand.

Dani gives up her phone.

41

"Okay," Beth says forty minutes later. "We have a lawyer. A Boston lawyer. We're going to his office Monday morning, and he agrees that you're to have no contact with anyone in case there's a further leak. So no school, no e-mail, no phone, nothing, until he gets this sewn up. He's going to call the police department today and start pressuring them to stop the leaks. 'Drum tight,' he's saying. He'll seal this drum tight. You're not a juvenile anymore so your age doesn't help, but the fact that the cops made a promise and broke it gives us some leverage. He thinks Pinto is in some kind of violation. I'm not allowed to discuss the case either, but I'm not going into hiding because I have some big sales calls this weekend and I'm planning to keep them. If anyone brings up the newspaper article I'll just ignore them and change the subject."

Dani decides not to show Beth the comments. They're not meant for Beth, anyway; they're meant for Dani. The meanest part inside these people is speaking to the meanest part of her.

42

Friday, May 14

Hawthorne *Beacon-Times*

DELL FAMILIES MEET ON SITTER DANGER

HAWTHORNE—

Parents in the Dell Place neighborhood—reeling in the wake of a babysitter's confession that she graphically visualized the murder of a five-year-old—met in a parent's home last night to discuss the news and formulate a response plan.

The mother of the child involved in the incident was "still in shock" after the sitter's revelation, she told the group. Her name is being withheld to protect the identity of the minor child. The babysitter's identity has not yet been released by police, who said there was no probable cause on which to press charges.

Host parent Noah Hurley expressed frustration that the babysitter has not been identified. "This is all about the kids' safety," said Hurley. "The well-being of our children is the ultimate issue that any of us cares about. I don't understand why we can't be told who this person is, just for our own protection."

Neighbor Liz Peña told a reporter invited to the meeting that if she were in the parent's place she would "stop at nothing" to protect her seven-year-old twins, Emma and Edith, who once attended a birthday party of the threatened child.

Hawthorne Police community safety officer Andrea Foale gave a presentation on babysitter safety at the parent meeting. She said the best precautions against abuse by a babysitter are obtaining references, watching the sitter interact with your child during an initial interview, and requesting a criminal record, or CORI, check.

Comments:

Coastal160 wrote:

So we know Nutjob Nanny wasn't working for the Hurleys or Peñas—who else lives in Dell Place?

Waster wrote:

That neighborhood is crawling with kids. Drive over 25mph any time of day or night and you'll hit a few of them.

St_jude wrote:

My heart goes out to this family, whoever they may be. That poor little boy and his parents, what a trauma . . . You are in our prayers.

Rowdie wrote:

That's Northeast liberalism for you. Where else in the world do they let crazed teen killers go free?

Coastal160 wrote:

HPD decided NN was "troubled."

Waster wrote:

There are some very nice juvenile detention facilities where she can get all the trouble she can handle.

peewe wrote:

Whos ready to form a lynchmob . . . Ive got a strong rope here you pick the tree.

Rowdie wrote:

Do it now, before a real tragedy occurs. So who is the babysitter?

Sheepdogg wrote:

I told you. I know, but I can't say.

43

"Hey." Meghan glides toward Shelley on the way to Hawtones. She wears a turquoise halter top fastened with a gold ring.

"Hey," Shelley says. "I really like that top on you. Where did you get it?"

The top isn't Shelley's style, but she feels that she has to explain her staring at Meghan by pretending she wants the same clothes.

"The beach store." Meghan shakes her armload of gold bangles. They jingled all during the movie last week, but Shelley didn't mind. Despite Dani's advice, she's going to invite Meghan for an ice cream after school.

"You always look great," Shelley says.

"So where's your friend today?" Meghan asks. "Dani skipping rehearsal?"

"She didn't come to school. I haven't heard from her."

"I hope she's not sick," Meghan says, smiling.

Shelley slows her athletic pace to match Meghan's swaying walk.

"I hope nothing's wrong," Meghan continues.

"I don't know if anything's wrong," Shelley says. "I haven't heard from her in the last twenty-four hours."

"It's getting dangerous in this town, with crazed babysitters around and whatnot. You know, a lot of people seem to think it's Dani."

"Dani would never do something like that," Shelley says. "What evidence do they have?"

"Word seems to have leaked out. People who know people who know people."

Shelley continues defending Dani, but even to her the defense feels weak. She sent Dani a bunch of text messages that went from voyeuristic glee: "Can you believe what's going on? I can't believe you're not in school!"

To stomach-sick suspicion: "Hey, doesn't Alex live on Dell Place?"

She's been thinking how nervous Dani acted when they talked about Mr. Gabler. She wants to believe it isn't Dani. Why doesn't Dani call her, or come to school?

"It is her," Meghan says, adjusting her halter outside the music room. "I thought she was weird because she fidgeted so much and always wore the same hoodie, but I didn't say so because I didn't want to hurt your feelings."

Shelley stops Meghan at the door.

"All right," she says. "I'm going to ask her point-blank if it's her or not. Dani would never lie to me. If she says no, then I'll know it's not her."

Down the hall someone screams like a kid being stabbed, and others clap and laugh. Someone else imitates a kid being strangled.

"Where's Dani this morning?" Nathan Brandifield asks when Shelley steps into the music room.

After school Shelley sends Dani one more message:

"People think it might be you. Tell me it isn't."

44

Dani begs Beth to let her check messages.

"I won't send any back, I promise."

"No phone."

"Mom, I'm going nuts. Just let me look. How would you feel with no connection to the outside world?"

"All right. But only five minutes. Just to check. No information goes to anyone about anything. The only person you can talk to is me."

Dani has two messages from Gordy: "Want to run tomorrow?" and "Hey, you're not in school. Are you all right?"

She has twelve messages from Shelley: "Can you believe what's going on? Where are you? I need to talk to you. Call me right away, okay? Meghan and I are at Icey's. I don't believe it could be you. I can't believe it."

She hands Beth the phone.

"Good girl," Beth says.

45

"Still no word," Shelley tells Meghan. "What should I do? I'm sure Dani can explain all these suspicions."

"You're in denial," Meghan says. She frowns and rests her chin on her hands. "I know it's tough accepting something like this."

"I guess you're right," Shelley says, "but this is practically the first time since we were little that I haven't talked to Dani. I wonder if I should stop at her house or something. I feel like I'm losing my best friend." She twists a straw wrapper until it breaks.

Meghan touches Shelley's fingertips. "I can be your new best friend," she says.

46

The Dogghouse
Sniffing Out That Babysitter
Your blog host: Sheepdogg
Rumors circling around about the identity of the Babysitter. One is that she's a deformed outcast who wanders around upscale neighborhoods carrying a butcher knife in a knapsack, peeking in the windows for children to kill. Another is that she cruises the supermarket parking lots for mothers with toddlers so she can ask if they need help with the stroller. Another is that she always wears a sweatshirt because the shirt underneath is bloodstained. Another is that once the parents leave she shows the kiddies a gun and says she'll kill them if they don't behave. Then she makes them sit for hours without moving or talking, and if they make even a peep she puts the barrel of the gun next to their head and pulls the trigger. Sort of like the Russian roulette scene in *The Deer Hunter*.

Well, none of those rumors are true. The babysitter is not an outcast. She is popular. She is also pretty. (Sheepdogg has seen her.) She's never killed anyone before. And it's definitely a knife, not a gun.

Who knows all this? Sheepdogg knows.

47

Saturday morning Dani sleeps late. Beth is working till two, and she's taken Dani's phone. In pajama pants and a tank top, Dani eats cereal and looks at the MyFace pages of her friends who have normal lives. She doesn't post anything or answer e-mails. She watches music videos until she hears someone at the front door.

She peers through the curtains and sees Gordy knocking. He's bare-chested, with his T-shirt tied around his waist. Beth said no phone, no e-mail, and no leaving the house, Dani reminds herself. She never said anything about visitors.

"Hey," Dani says, giving Gordy a peck on the cheek. "Quick. Come in."

"I hope you don't mind," Gordy says, pulling on his red T-shirt as he enters the hall. "I called you a few times about joining me, but I didn't hear back."

"That's because I'm grounded," Dani says.

"No phone, either?"

"That's right."

"Should I ask why?"

"Because I talk too much. I said a bunch of stuff I shouldn't have said. Keep calling, though. I can't call out, but I can still check messages."

"That sounds medieval."

"It's fair under the circumstances."

"My dad knows your mom a little. He says she's a nice lady."

"She is. And we're really close. But anyway, under the circumstances it's best if you only stay a short time. I'm glad for the company, though."

"It's great outside. I was going to invite you to my house. We could sit in papasan chairs and eat Indian food and watch the ocean. Maybe when you're ungrounded. We need to practice. Should we get right to it?"

They run through two songs. Then they mimic Nathan Brandifield—his singing, his instrument imitations, and the way he walks—until they feel bad about it. Dani serves microwave burritos and Vitaminwater.

"I want you to know that I've heard weird stuff at school," Gordy says while they're clearing the dishes, "and I don't believe any of it."

"I don't want to talk about that," Dani says. She was having so much fun until this second. Now this morning, too, is tainted.

"Anyway I think it's far more likely that Nathan Brandifield is the babysitter."

Dani pretends to be distracted by the dishwasher.

"I'm sorry, that was mean," Gordy says. "I was trying to make you laugh."

"Look," Dani says, shutting off the dishwasher and closing the cupboards.

Gordy looks out the kitchen window at the swimming pool and fountain.

"I meant 'Look, I'm about to say something.'"

"All right." Her face is sideways to him. She can feel him staring at her ear as though it's the most important ear in the world.

"This isn't a good time for me to be seeing somebody. For the next couple of months, at least."

Gordy waits for her to say more. She's wearing a tank top, pj bottoms, and flip-flops, and although she hadn't gone to any trouble to look nice, she realizes from the way he's watching her that she might be sensational-looking and never need to change anything visual about herself. It's a great realization, but it comes at a bad time. If it had come at a better time she would have rolled it into a corner of her mind like a sacred ball.

"Is it because I made fun of Nathan? I know you guys are friendly."

"No, I imitated him too."

"Then I don't understand. Look, I told you I don't believe any of those rumors."

"I need to be by myself for a while."

"Because of what happened with your mom? Because you're grounded?"

"Even aside from being grounded."

Dani turns around. Gordy's lower lip is trembling. She's studied that lip carefully over the school year. It's pretty muscular from playing the French horn, so in her texts to Shelley she calls it his MLL: muscular lower lip. Gordy looks so vulnerable right now.

Dani thinks about his insides being on the outside. She squeezes her hands together.

"All right," he says. "I'm not going to push you. Just tell me, will you call me if you ever change your mind? If the time is right?"

To lose him so soon after losing Alex—Dani feels bereft. She opens the back door. "Sneak out this way," she says. "Thanks for coming by and cheering me up."

"Or don't call me," he says on the back patio. He smiles bravely. "Send me a secret signal. I'll know it when I hear it."

48

At four thirty Beth calls the house phone. Dani assumes she's allowed to pick up.

"What's going on?" Dani asks. "I thought you'd be home by now. It's too quiet." She's sincere about the quiet, though she'll never tell Beth that Gordy was here.

"Work is going well, but"—Beth lowers her voice to a whisper—"the other thing is going very badly."

Dani's heart pounds. "Where are you? No one knows, do they? From what I can tell, they don't seem to know."

"I'm in my car. I don't know why I'm whispering. It's just that this thing is the only thing people talk about. And I'm acting like I know nothing about it, but that looks suspicious too. So I don't know how much to say. God, I wish it were Monday!"

"I'm sorry, Mom."

Beth is silent. She's probably changing lanes on the highway. "It may be my fault as much as yours. I don't know."

"Have you told Sean?" Dani asks her.

"I'm not telling Sean anything. I've told him I can't see him for a few days because you're having teenage problems. Okay, I'll be home in half an hour."

Dani lies on the couch. She and Shelley always hated being indoors. If there was a thunderstorm, they'd go to the beach and watch the waves. If there was a blizzard, they'd build a fort.

She checks the Internet again. There's a new editorial in the *Beacon-Times*.

49

Saturday, May 15

Editorial

PUBLIC: GIVE US THE NAME

In the short time since the *Beacon-Times* ran a story about a teenage Hawthorne babysitter who revealed to police that she had murderous thoughts about a boy in her care, our office has been inundated with phone calls, e-mails, and visits from readers insisting that we name the sitter. Readers have used the phrase "the public's right to know," citing safety concerns and risks to the community. However, the Hawthorne Police Department has made a compelling case that the incident is under control. Since no crime was committed and the girl in question has obeyed the police's insistence that she seek treatment from a mental health professional, the *Beacon-Times* has respected the department's request that the teen's identity not be revealed.

To make a judgment call that disagreed with the wishes of a large number of our readers was not easy, and our editorial board did not arrive at this decision lightly. But our final assessment was that curiosity does not equal the right to know. Those who disagree should consider that some of our callers and correspondents also insisted on being told the names of both the five-year-old child and the child's mother. The identities of both parties, of course, are protected due to the minor status of the child involved.

During the past forty-eight hours the *Beacon-Times* and its editors have been accused of yielding to the undue influence of family connections. Some readers have insisted that if the girl in question were from a poor family rather than a prosperous one, or were new in town rather than socially well connected, her name would have appeared in the paper immediately. But the *Beacon-Times* has established guidelines for revealing the identities of people in the community, and we have hewn to those guidelines in this case as we have in every case since 1995.

We hope that readers who are angry or disappointed at our decision keep in mind that someday they could be at the fringe—or even the center—of a newsworthy event, and the *Beacon-Times* would be equally judicious in deciding how much to reveal about that story.

Comments:

Beavis wrote:

The *Beacon-Times* is worried about getting sued, and

that is the whole reason behind their journalistic imperative, period.

Waster wrote:
Youre right its money period.

Dani hears Beth's key in the door. She smells Chinese food.

"Who wants kung pao chicken?" Beth asks. When Dani doesn't answer, Beth comes to the couch and reads over Dani's shoulder.

"All right," Beth says when she reaches the end of the comments. "I'm calling Boston to see if we can go in earlier."

She goes to her office, then comes back in a few minutes to say the lawyer can't see them on Sunday because he's playing golf.

"I could speak to someone in town," Beth says while they're eating. "I could get some local advice to tide us over. But given all that's going around"—she points at Dani's laptop—"I don't think that's a good idea."

Beth gives Dani five minutes with her phone. Dani hears Gordon asking her to go for a run this morning.

"That boy?" Beth asks. "You really like him?"

Dani nods, handing the phone back. Her eyes feel teary.

"When this is over, honey," Beth says. "All in good time."

"He said his dad met you and thinks you're nice."

"When did he say that?" Beth asks.

Oops, Dani thinks. "Last time I talked to him," she says, which is true.

"Dani," Beth says that night at bedtime, "is there anything

you've been telling Dr. Kumar that I should know? Anything I should hear that would help me understand?"

Dani shakes her head no. "Thanks for looking after me, Mom," she says.

Beth goes into her room and locks the door.

50

Sunday morning Beth makes pancakes and bacon.

"Gotta keep our strength up, right?" she says. She's going to work today, because Sunday is the biggest day in real-estate sales and because, clearly, she wants to. "I want to look as normal as possible. And I hope people have found something else to talk about by now," Beth says.

Dani wishes she could get out and do something too.

"You'll be all right, won't you?" Beth asks Dani. "Can you avoid getting bored?"

"I'll poke around online," Dani says. "And there's always homework."

Beth gives Dani five minutes on the phone.

A message came in from Gordy last night:

"Look, I'm sorry to call so soon after you sent me away. I just want to be sure you're all right."

And another one this morning: "I completely missed what you tried to say yesterday. Is this why you stopped babysitting? Please can you call me?"

"I'll check in this afternoon," Beth says. "You can pick up the phone when I call."

It's a warm day in the middle of May, so Dani puts on a sundress and flip-flops. She pours more coffee and gives herself a pedicure. While her toes are drying, she opens her laptop. Maybe Beth is right, and people found something else to talk about. The *Beacon-Times* has no new stories about the Babysitter, but forty more people have commented on the editorial.

> Coastal160 wrote:
> Did anyone see a cruiser in front of the Solomons' house on Highgate Road Friday?
>
> Sanddollar wrote:
> I saw Beth Solomon in the market this a.m. She had on big honking sunglasses and a headscarf like she was Mary-Kate Olsen or somebody.
>
> Sheepdogg wrote:
> Nice sighting, Sanddollar. Check out my blog, The-DoggHouse, for breaking news.
>
> Waster wrote:
> BetSo hot! Dani not so hot! Must take after the old man.
>
> MPthree wrote:
> She's all right. I would do her no problem but you'd have to watch your back the whole time.

All right, they know, Dani says to herself. *Everybody knows.*

51

What to do? It would be fine, Dani decides, to write an e-mail and not send it, to save it as a draft and let Beth press Send if she decided it was okay. Dani's hands shake. She has trouble keeping her fingers on the keyboard.

> Dear Dad,
>
> How are you? I hope this is still your correct address. If it bounces back I'll do a search or I'll ask Mom if she has it. I suppose I could send snail mail, but this issue is rather time-sensitive so I don't think I have time.
>
> What I want to ask is, how would you feel about me coming to stay for a while? Maybe a few months, or maybe longer. Since summer is coming, I don't have to worry about school. Mom would pay my plane fare and I could get some kind of job out there to pay for my own expenses. Maybe I could be a whitewater guide or something like that.

Dani rereads her message while one finger hovers on the Delete key. Her dad and Julia won't want her around their kids. In fact she should avoid kids for a while; maybe the rest of her life.

Dani closes her laptop. She curls on the couch, trying to devise a strategy. A lot of people who liked her before are going to hate her now. She doesn't know where she'll be able to hide if not here. She tries to push away a belief that some kind of punishment is inevitable, the natural cause-and-effect outcome of having these bad thoughts.

52

The Dogg House
Sniffing Out That Babysitter
Your blog host: Sheepdogg
Out of Sight, Out of Mind?
Word on the street is that the Babyslitter, I mean Babysitter, is hiding at home in the swank neighborhood of Ocean View. She was not seen in public either Friday or Saturday. Does she believe that if she doesn't show her face, this will go away . . . *poof*?

Sheepdogg knows.

To Sheepdogg:
Just a private note of encouragement from a group of fans in another part of the country. We are a national clearinghouse for crimes that are underattended by local law enforcement. We like the way you are going about writing on this case. Please look at our website; we'd love for you to check us out.
Rowdie
POK (Protect Our Kids)

To Rowdie:

Thanks for the props. Working hard on the blog without much feedback. My dad is a cop, really frustrated. I'm very interested in your group. Stay in touch. Would like to visit sometime, btw. Montana looks phenomenal!

To Sheepdogg:

How would you like to be our eyes and ears in Hawthorne?

53

The landline rings while Dani's on the computer. It rings seven times, twelve times, twenty-two times. Dani's mom would never let the phone ring twenty-two times.

On her e-mail Dani has a message from MyFace.com saying "Check out the new girl in town!" It sends her to her own profile page.

54

MyFace Profile

Name: Dani Death

"Aspiring kiddie killer"

Sex: Female

Age: 17 years old

Location: Hawthorne, Massachusetts, United States

Last log-in: May 16

Mood: cold

Interested in:

General: being crazy

Sounds: human screaming, blood gurgling from an open wound

Movies: *Finding Nemo Hacked to Pieces*

About me: I am a psychotic bitch who thinks about killing kids. How about I watch yours while you go to the movies? Don't rush home and don't bother calling—everything is JUST FINE.

Who I'd like to meet: your local kindergarten.

55

Dani hears a car in the driveway. She shouldn't go to the door unless she knows it's Beth. She stands in the living room and tries to peer out the picture window. It's a bright blue May day. She moves the curtain slowly, so no one will detect her. She hears a crash and something hard comes through the plate glass, getting caught in the curtain. The car's horn blares like someone's leaning on it, as intrusive and unstoppable a noise as the twenty-two rings, as the driver takes off in a spray of gravel.

The object lies on the carpet surrounded by shards of glass as large as Dani's hand. It's a stone the size of a baseball, wrapped in a piece of paper secured by rubber bands. Dani snaps off the bands, unfolds the paper, and reads

DIE KIDDIE KILLER

56

Dani dials Shelley's number.

"It was you!" Shelley says. "You're the babysitter. I can't believe it, Dani."

"Are you home? Can I come over now?" Dani asks. "Can I stay at your house for a few days?"

"Are you kidding? My mom would never have you in the house. How could you treat Alex that way?"

"I never did anything. I only thought about doing it. That's what I needed to tell you that day. That was my secret. I had a secret, just like you have a secret."

"My secret is nothing like your secret, Dani."

Dani hears the dial tone.

57

Dani tries to stuff things into her pack. Her hands shake so much that they slow her down. She calls her mother and the voice mail message comes on, soothing, cajoling, and full of confidence. "You've reached Beth Solomon of Solomon and Cahill Properties . . ."

"Mom, I have to go!" she yells. "They're after me."

She runs the same way she sent Gordon, out the back door, past the fountain, and into the woods.

58

Sunday, May 16

MONSTER

says the headline in the National Envestigator News Online. Below that word is a photo of Dani from the Hawthorne *Beacon-Times* sports page, cropped to show only her head and shoulders. She has hit the ball out of bounds and has a disgusted expression on her face. Blown up to six inches, the picture looks angry and deranged. Like the face of a monster.

part 4 THE WOODS

59

Protect Our Kids

Chat Room

SHEEPDOGG: Problem solved, Rowdie. Dani Death is gone. Since yesterday.

ROWDIE: Where is she now?

SHEEPDOGG: Don't know just yet, but we've got her on the run. I'll sniff around. Maybe once we flushed her out she got whacked by an irate parent.

ROWDIE: Too bad the cops don't have the cojones to handle that girl. Cops aren't good for much other than speeding tickets.

SHEEPDOGG: Not their fault. They wanted to lock her up but their hands were tied. Anyway, I heard that when BetSo got home from selling McMansions her lil darlin was gone.

ROWDIE: That's right. She escaped Hawthorne and is off to some other town to chop babies into Tater Tots!

SHEEPDOGG: What do we do now, assuming she remains at large?

ROWDIE: POK will list her in its offender registry and post her picture in all the surrounding towns.

We'll get the word out to POK Massachusetts and POK New Hampshire. And we'll keep working our media contacts. Somebody will find her.

SHEEPDOGG: Bell rang. Gotta go. Check in later.

ROWDIE: Good dog!

60

Dear Alex,

It's hard for me to write this. You must be confused, since one minute I was there and the next I was gone. I don't know what you've been told about me or by whom, but I want you to know that I never really wanted to hurt you. Just the opposite—I wanted to keep you safe.

I shouldn't tell you any of this since I think little kids should be protected from bad things. Remember how I wanted the TV off when something scary came on? I wanted to protect you. Anyway, by now you probably know that there's something wrong with me and that's why I had to leave.

I got the idea of writing this because I saw some berries growing and wondered how Louie was doing. You take such good care of him. Someday you'll take care of someone the same way I wanted to take care of you.

Now I wonder why I'm even writing this. You can't read some of these words. And who would read them to you? Not your mom, I'm sure. Anyway, I'll just say I'm thinking of you. No one will ever see this, but here is my thought of you, written down on paper and buried under a maple tree.

Love always,

Dani

61

"Is that Big Red?" the elderly woman asks. Her husband is reading the paper. The front-page photo looks like the tall tennis-playing redhead from across the street. "Got another win, did she?"

"No." Her husband, Jonas, hands her the front section. The headline of the *Beacon-Times* says TROUBLED TEEN GOES MISSING. So this must be why the cruiser was there. She and Jonas had looked the other way to avoid causing embarrassment.

She remembers Big Red and her friend the brunette as children coming home from tennis lessons in their white outfits. She recalls how things were across the street when Beth's husband moved to Colorado. The yard wasn't maintained, but Big Red and her friend would connect the sprinkler and run through it, leaping over the highest weeds. When Beth brought Big Red for trick-or-treating that year she was a big girl, but she wore her princess costume from the previous year, which was too short and tight. Jonas tried to tease Big Red by saying there was no candy, but she saw the candy dish and opened the front door and went right for it. "That's our Big Red," her husband would say any time her tennis scores appeared. After a while Beth added the pool and the girls didn't need the sprinkler anymore.

"Life can be very hard," the woman says, handing the paper to her husband.

"It certainly can be," he says.

"Poor Big Red," she says.

Her husband turns to the next article. "Right for the candy dish," he says, and they both chuckle.

62

Shelley can't wrap her mind around the idea of Dani being dangerous and psycho. It's too extreme. Instead Shelley dwells on the fact that her best friend is gone, in one way or another, and Shelley can no longer talk to her.

Every day since they were little kids, Shelley and Dani talked, even when Dani took that trip to Colorado. There was always this person, a strong, reliable wall to bounce her thoughts off of. Someone who could make her feel normal. *I'll talk to my best friend*, Shelley told herself when something was discouraging or upsetting or just plain tangled.

That's why, out of everyone in the world, Dani was the one Shelley came out to. She knew her parents were not the right people—they had left their previous church because the church voted to allow gay ministers. Her brother was not the right one—he was just a little kid. GSA was all wrong, because even though it's a gay-support group, Shelley considers it her safe place to hide. She hasn't wanted to draw attention to herself there.

Being secretly gay had felt like a burden she needed to be rid of. She set a deadline for when she would tell Dani, but the conditions were never perfect. Dani was distracted by something else, they were interrupted, or someone might overhear. So Shelley set a second deadline. And then she ended up blurting her secret in the courtyard at lunchtime just to get it over with.

When Shelley was little she told her parents she was going to marry Dani. Ha, ha, ha, they'd said, that's not right. They had guests over, so they treated it as a joke, one of those funny mistakes kids make.

"No, it's true," she'd said. "I do want to marry Dani."

"Shush," her mother said angrily. "You can't marry a girl. That's wrong. You have to pick a boy." Their reaction was so strong that Shelley never said anything like that again.

And actually, she was never attracted to Dani the way she was later to other girls. She had said it only because they were so comfortable together, true best friends. She was attracted to a different kind of girl—the flirty, social girls who put their looks out there more than she and Dani did.

At first she tried to convince herself that she merely admired or envied these girls. She paid obsessive attention to the girls she thought were pretty: the clothes they wore, the friends they had, the boys they dated. She could try to imitate them if she wanted. She could try to look and act the way they did. But then she had to admit that she didn't want to be like them. She wanted to be with them.

Of course I'm not gay, she told herself many times. *Both boys and girls like to look at girls, because girls look better. They take better care of themselves. They make sure their clothes fit right and their skin smells good.* And in Meghan's case, who of either orientation wouldn't want to be around her? The way she moved, her easy manner of chatting people up. But once Shelley admitted to Dani that she was gay, she could accept her true feelings about Meghan. She was falling in love with her.

Now the only person who knows who Shelley really is has disappeared. It's as if Shelley never even came out to Dani. As if her gayness and her secret love were dropped into the ocean fathoms down. The one person she was ever completely comfortable with is someone she will never talk to, not ever again.

63

Dani walked all last night, assuming it was safest to be on the move. Her feet are sore from the stones and gravel poking into her flip-flops, and her face, neck, and legs are welted with bug bites. She peers through the branches at Havenswood's sparkling reservoir. She would love to step into it, but it's the town's water supply. If she can find a receptacle she can carry some away to drink and wash with. She sees a Shane's Supermarket bag and kicks it open to make sure it hasn't been used for dog poop. She dips the bag into the water and watches it fill.

Dani goes back into the woods with her pack and water pouch, staying close to the trees in case she needs to hide. She hears traffic on Route 133. She wonders who threw that rock with the message—Mrs. Alex? Mrs. Alex's friends? The police? A stranger?—and how soon they'll find her. She has little experience with hiding. She wishes she had paid more attention to books and movies that discussed clues like trampled grass.

She'll need to sleep tonight. While it's light she finds the Shark's Jaw boulder she stood on with Gordy. The hollow between the jaws will be her base. She hangs her bag of water on a tree and gathers armloads of leaves to pad the crevice. She has only her summer dress and hoodie to wear. She should have brought food, running shoes, pants, a T-shirt, a towel.

She wonders what Beth thought when she found the rock and saw Dani was gone. Beth must be trying to find her. She wishes Beth wouldn't worry. In a way she's glad that the person who threw the rock drove her out of Hawthorne. For the first time in months, she feels relaxed. She doesn't have to touch her mouth or squeeze her hands together. *They did me a favor*, she thinks. *Finally, I can't hurt anyone.*

64

Protect Our Kids

Member Alerts

New message from: Rowdie

Attention, POK Mass and NH!

What can you do to protect kids in Hawthorne?

1. Hang this Dani Solomon Potential Child Killer poster everywhere you can. It includes contact info for state and national POK.

2. Call police chief at H. station EVERY 10 MINS and demand DD apprehension. Name is Scola 1-978-555-6530

3. Sheepdogg to distribute phone numbers of entire HHS junior and senior class, music groups, tennis team. Call assigned numbers to see if DD staying there. OK to say you are reporter from Hawthorne *Beacon-Times* or any newspaper or large media. Offer any payment or reward you want—not necessary to actually pay anyone!

POK over police

We care about community

65

Monday, May 17

Hawthorne *Beacon-Times*

Opinion

By Cecilia Martin

HAWTHORNE'S WARNING

A student, one of our own, has been questioned about her possible intent to harm a very young child, and has now disappeared. Educators and parents in our community are asking themselves, How well do we know the kids we teach? How well do we know the kids we raise? And how did this situation progress so far without anyone knowing?

Dani Solomon is an honor student, a star athlete, a promising musician, and a very popular young lady. But she fooled all of us. Because deep inside, allegedly, is someone very different. Now we are shaken by how close to tragedy our community may have come.

Our schools need to do a much better job of finding the Dani Solomons that lurk behind an appealing facade. We can do this by conducting psychological assessments on each incoming high school student at the beginning of freshman year. We can do it by establishing a "see something, say something" policy by which all students become mandated reporters of suspicious activity by their fellow students. Complying with this policy can be tied to the school honor code. We can do it by following the lead of other communities and installing metal detectors at the entrance to each educational facility. And we can do it with periodic random locker searches. Students may complain about lack of privacy with these new measures, but who knows what tragedies may be averted?

The life that is saved may be your own.

Cecilia Martin is an instructor of English at Hawthorne High School.

66

Malcolm sets his phone ID to "unavailable." He says he's calling from an organization that finds missing children.

"Is Dani Solomon staying there? You can tell me. I'm asking because I may be able to help. Well then, do you know where she might be? Did she reveal any plans to you before she left? Has she been in touch with you since Sunday?"

But Shelley's parents don't let her come to the phone, and the rest of the kids he calls don't know any more than what they read on the Internet. No one has seen her since the day her picture came out in the paper. But Malcolm imitated his dad's tone in order to sound older, and he's pleased that no one recognized his voice.

67

Text messages, Meghan and Shelley:

"You looked distracted today, chiquita."

"Thinking about Dani. I got calls from a newspaper and a missing-persons bureau last night, asking me if I knew where she was. It's all so weird, isn't it?"

"Just as well that she's gone. Think of the danger you were in. She's crazy. She could have hurt YOU!"

"That would have bothered you?"

"Absolutely. Don't you think you matter to me? Sometimes I think it would have been so easy to let this school year go by without getting to know you. I'm really glad that didn't happen."

68

Voice mail on Dani's phone:

Beth: I don't know why I'm leaving a message here since I have your phone, but I need to know where you are.

Sean: She can't hear you, Beth. Why don't you give me the phone?

Beth: I wish I hadn't taken your phone. I only wanted to make sure you didn't get in more trouble than you already got yourself in. Now I don't even know whether you're alive.

Sean: Beth, she can't hear you. Come on, give me the phone and let's go to bed.

Beth: I wish I hadn't taken your phone. Why did I do that?

69

"I wish Dani didn't move away," Alex says Tuesday morning, while Mrs. Alex helps him dress for school.

"But she did," replies Mrs. Alex.

"Can we send a letter to Dani and ask her to move back?"

"We don't need Dani. We have April now."

"April doesn't like me."

"Of course she does."

"She said I was a brat."

"Try not to make April mad and she won't call you names."

Alex knew Dani didn't always do everything right. Sometimes she looked worried and didn't pay enough attention to Alex, and sometimes she talked to her friend Shelley on the phone. A couple of times he couldn't fall asleep and he called for her and it took a long while for Dani to come up because she was doing her homework.

Mrs. Alex told Alex he had to let Dani do her homework. "Stop being selfish, Alex" was exactly what she said. Maybe that was the reason Dani moved away, because he was too selfish.

70

When Dani wakes she's cold. A pink glow underlies the blue-gray sky. She brushes something from her lower leg. The short dress makes her feel vulnerable, like a snake, lizard, or weasel might slink underneath it. She pulls the blanket up to her neck and tries to sleep some more.

Blanket. Where has this blanket come from? It's not a sleeping bag but a definite indoor blanket. Ivory material with little flowers and gold trim, like something a mom or grandmom would have on her bed. It's already dirty. She hadn't heard a sound. Who got close enough to wrap a blanket around her?

She gets up and finds a cloth supermarket bag. Inside are a ground sheet, a two-liter bottle of water, a plastic cup, a spoon, trail mix and cereal bars, a jar of peanut butter, and three apples. She looks for a note but finds none.

Dani washes her crotch and armpits with her bottle of water. She thinks of Alex, who, despite Dani's watchfulness, saw part of a movie in which someone was stabbed in the bathroom—was it *Psycho*? Or *A Nightmare on Elm Street*? After that he asked her to stand in the hallway and talk to him anytime he peed. He thought she was his protector. She imagines his face in the moment of her murdering him. She imagines waking him up and saying, "I'm going to kill you." Him realizing in the last seconds of his life that he was wrong; she's not his protector. Here in the woods she has no way to hurt Alex. That's good. But she has no way to check on him either. If only she were in touch with Beth. She could ask her to drive past his house and see if he's okay.

She'll walk around again today. Then maybe tonight the people who threw the rock will find her. Or the coyotes will come looking for her. Either way it would be for the best. Dani Solomon could run forever and she would still have the thoughts. It would be better for everyone if Dani Solomon never went back home.

71

Shelley finds a note in her locker:

"I hope your day is better than yesterday."

It has a heart drawn at the bottom.

72

The Dogg House

Sniffing Out That Babysitter

Your blog host: Sheepdogg

No one seems to know the whereabouts of Dani Solomon. But we all know that if someone truly wants to go missing, there is only one place in Hawthorne to hide.

73

Gordy gets a call on his landline from a newspaper offering to pay him for information about Dani. Then he gets a call on his cell phone that appears to be from Dani, but instead it's Dani's mother, asking if he has any idea who she might be staying with. "If you know where she is but you're not allowed to tell me," Beth asks, "at least let me know she's safe."

Gordy says he's sorry, but he doesn't know anything. "I wish we could have met under other circumstances," he tells Beth before she hangs up.

74

To: Rowdie

From: Sheepdogg

No breaks yet. But I suggest you try Havenswood.

75

Message on Dani Death's MyFace page:

I WILL DO EVERYTHING IN MY POWER TO HELP YOU AND PROTECT YOU.

PLEASE COME HOME.

MOM

76

Malcolm Pinto and his father sit in front of the TV with a plate of nachos.

"Here it comes," says Officer Pinto. "Turn it up louder."

Malcolm raises the volume with the remote.

"Oh my God, look at them all," Pinto says. The town is holding a press conference for the Boston news media.

Sergeant Mason stands up first. He's wearing his dress uniform with the blazer and hat, the same one he wears in parades.

"Color me douche," says Pinto. Malcolm laughs.

"Thank you for taking the time from your busy investigative schedules"—some of the reporters laugh at that—"to be with us today. This is going to be short and sweet. Daniela Solomon has not been charged with any crime. She is not being sought in connection with any crime. Daniela Solomon is being sought as a missing person, in the interests of her own safety, not because of any involvement in a crime." He glances at the police chief, who motions to him to sit down.

"Lap dog," Pinto comments. Malcolm makes a panting noise.

Beth Solomon stands up next.

"Whoa, BetSo is bringing it," Pinto says. "Look at that little suit."

"She looks so commanding," Malcolm agrees. "Like she's president or something."

Beth glances at a prosperous-looking man beside her.

"He must be her lawyer," Pinto says. "Boston, probably. Big bucks there."

"My daughter, Daniela, has the same rights as any citizen of Hawthorne, of Massachusetts, and of the United States," Beth begins. "If you are a parent"—she looks right into the camera—"you understand some of the pain and anxiety that Dani's departure has caused me."

"Dani caused someone pain," says Pinto. "Shocker."

"Dani, please come home," Beth says, her eyes watering into the camera like she's on a Lifetime special. "You don't have to be afraid to come back to Hawthorne. We can work everything out. There are people who will help us. Coming home is the first step."

"Look at those three," Officer Pinto says, pointing to a woman and two men in the audience, all wearing camouflage. "This is bringing a lot of weirdos to town." One of the men holds a sign above his head saying PROTECT OUR KIDS. Malcolm realizes that this must be the New Hampshire contingent. He wonders if he should tell his father that he's been corresponding with POK. But he doesn't for now, because he likes having something of his own.

Now Chief Scola stands up. "It's just one bad decision after another for that guy," says Officer Pinto. The chief was responsible for Mason making sergeant rather than Pinto.

"While the Hawthorne Police Department appreciates the interest so many media outlets have shown in our town and in the Dani Solomon case, the proliferation of media representatives in what is normally a very quiet town is making it difficult for us to fulfill our responsibilities, one of which is finding Dani Solomon. There is no story here. We would like you all to pack up and go back to wherever it is you came from. Once again, there is no story. We are prepared to prosecute to the full extent of the law any media representatives that trespass on private property or harass local people for information."

A reporter from Channel 5 raises his hand. "Chief Scola, what is the legal status of remarks like Dani's? Are they a threat? A warning? A confession?"

"I can't comment," the chief says.

Beth Solomon pops back up and looks straight into the camera. "I have one more thing to say," she says. "If anyone out there thinks that for any reason it's okay to hurt my daughter, know that I will go to the ends of the earth to find you and . . ." Her lawyer pulls her jacket to make her sit down.

"Scary!" Pinto says.

"That's where Dani gets it from," Malcolm adds.

The mayor approaches the microphone, but Michael Pinto kills the TV before she can speak. "They want our guys to stick their necks out?" he says. He calls some of his fellow officers.

77

The Dogg House

Sniffing Out That Babysitter

Your blog host: Sheepdogg

You heard it here first. The police are off the case. Hunting season has officially opened in Havenswood.

78

Wednesday, May 19

Hawthorne *Beacon-Times*

PRESS MEET LEADS TO

STRIFE OVER SITTER SEARCH

Following yesterday's press conference at which Hawthorne Police Department Sergeant Philip Mason stated that allegedly troubled babysitter Dani Solomon was "a missing person," rumors circulated that police plan a sick-out in protest of orders to search for Dani Solomon in Havenswood. A source close to department employees said that five of the seven officers assigned to tomorrow's search have already called in sick after stating privately that ensuring the teen's well-being is tantamount to "escorting the fox back to the henhouse." The source stated that the consensus among the officers is that if Solomon is sought it should be as a criminal rather than as a missing person.

Meanwhile, a spokesperson for the mother whom Dani Solomon allegedly warned about killing her child said that the mother and other area parents were "very concerned" about the fact that Dani Solomon was at large and that they would feel "more secure" if her whereabouts were known. They asked that the Hawthorne Police Department participate in a widespread search in order to protect local children.

"Considering that this is the first time in twenty years that Hawthorne has had a potential killer on its hands," said one parent who declined to be identified, "it seems ridiculous to drop the whole matter as if nothing happened."

79

Hawthorne *Beacon-Times*
Opinion
By Devorah Hopkins
CHANGING THE CONVERSATION

Be careful what you wish for, because you might get it. After years of effort by the Hawthorne Chamber of Commerce to attract visitors, Hawthorne is finally on the map. But for what are we known? Few residents have been spared this week the unflattering experience of being approached by journalists seeking information or opinions on the Dani Solomon case. The town has appeared on the Boston news upward of three times this week and once on the national news. And outside vendors have descended on our community hawking tasteless items such as T-shirts bearing the nickname "Sawthorne."

The only positive outcome of these events has been an uptick in business for Hawthorne's hotels and restaurants. But where are the photos of our scenic coastline and beaches? The stories about our maritime heritage? The glowing reports of our sports teams? Where are the accounts of concerts and dance performances and the valiant efforts of our struggling fishing fleet to stay afloat in uncertain economic times?

Remember, you and I set the tone for visitors to this town. If the Dani Solomon case is all we talk about, it's all visitors will hear. Let's all work on changing the conversation and showing the world that Hawthorne is a wonderful, safe place to vacation, raise children, work, and retire.

Devorah Hopkins is mayor of Hawthorne.

80

National Envestigator News

To: Photo Research Department

From: Editorial Department

Offer $1,000 to anyone in Hawthorne for a high-quality, high-res photo of Dani Solomon in a swimsuit.

81

To: Editorial Department

From: Photo Research Department

Which of these do you like?

82

National Envestigator News

IF LOOKS COULD KILL

Beautiful But Deadly Teen Sought

in Child Murder Case

Fugitive teen Dani Solomon, in hoodie over bikini, dances in front of a bonfire last summer at Hawthorne's Annual Fourth of July Picnic.

83

Only Gordy would know to look for her at the Shark's Jaw.

He brought her provisions and made sure she was okay. How did she look when he found her? Dani wonders. Did she stink, and was her eye half-closed from mosquito bites, like it is today? Did he think she was beautiful, or just pathetic? He'll probably come back to check on her again. She'll have to clean up a little in case he comes back. Then she can figure out how much he still likes her.

Why didn't he wake me up? she asks herself. *And why didn't he speak to me?* Because he's a kind person, but he's not an idiot. He wanted her to survive, but never in a million years would he still want to be her boyfriend. She must seem a lot different to him now than the day they walked here together. By now he's read the comments in the paper and seen her hacked MyFace profile. Before she left he said he didn't believe the rumors. Now he knows they're true. No way is Gordy coming back.

84

For the first time in five years, the Hawthorne girls' team has made it to the state semifinals. Dani was one of the players that put them there, but now Shelley is partnered with Justine Lamont. Justine is fast and a good strategist, but the communication Shelley shared with Dani is missing.

"We better shape up," Shelley says when it's Justine's turn to serve.

Justine sneers at Shelley.

"Sorry," Shelley says. "I meant *we* as in both of us. You're kinda touchy, aren't you?"

The Arlington Catholic High girls, twice in a row, lob balls into a spot where Justine is blinded by the sun.

"Hey, that happened last point too," Shelley says.

Justine throws her racket onto the court, and the lineswoman penalizes Justine for bad behavior.

85

Dani awakens to the soft hoot of an owl. She remembers that she's outside, that she's in Havenswood, that she ran away, that she left because of Alex, and that she can't hurt anyone anymore.

The owl's hoot is very musical. It takes Dani back to a music room, to being part of a circle, to making one note of a ringing chord. To a day when forgetting Shelley's sheet music was the worst problem she had. Wait—the owl is hooting "Old Cape Cod," so softly she can barely hear it. Her excellent guest must be here. *That means he knows about me—and he doesn't care.*

The owl comes closer. But—the owl isn't singing tenor, Gordy's part. The owl is singing baritone. Dani sees big white sneakers under the brush.

"Are you awake?" a voice whispers.

"Yes," Dani answers.

Nathan Brandifield parts the branches and sits down. He plunks a Whole Foods bag beside her pillow.

"Flashlight. Batteries. Pistachios. Oranges. Nonperishable milk. Straws, the bendy kind. Gummi Bears for quick energy. From the Hawtones."

It would be impolite to act disappointed. But now that she knows it's Nathan, she doesn't care about smelling bad.

"You brought me the blanket and the peanut butter," she whispers. "Thanks."

"You're welcome. I wasn't sure if you preferred chunky or smooth. That never arose in our previous conversations."

"I can't believe you did all this. I mean, you risked your safety. Why would you do such a thing?"

Nathan pushes his chin forward, like a childish scowl. "Why? Because we were worried about you. You're a Hawtone. You're part of the circle."

"How did you figure out where I was?"

"I've spent a lot of time in these woods. I knew Shark's Jaw was the primo location for someone to spend the night."

"Somebody threw a rock in my window. I think they want to kill me."

"I know. It's probably good you're not there. They painted slogans on your house, too. And there are reporters showing up every day and your mother has to shoo them away."

"And you say the Hawtones are worried about me? Which ones?"

"Shelley is having a rough time. But Meghan is helping her through it. Mr. Gabler is definitely worried. I think he wanted to save that part for you."

"Mr. Gabler cares about me? Still?"

"He's pretty unflappable. Do you know he's done music programs in prisons? He isn't afraid of anybody."

Dani blinks. That's right, people are afraid of her.

"I'm sorry, that was insensitive. Of course you're not going to prison. You know, it's hard to look at you and believe that stuff. But for a lot of people that makes the bad stuff more believable. That you're, you know, attractive. You know how people are." He puts her supplies back in the bag. "I could get you some chili and a can opener. Are you by any chance a vegetarian? If so, you never mentioned it."

"This should be enough." Dani doesn't have much to say to Nathan, but it's good to see another human being. *I could kill Nathan Brandifield,* she thinks. *I could bury him here and no one would find his body.* She squeezes her hands together. *Oh no. It's starting up again.*

"Are your hands cold?" Nathan asks. "Do you need gloves?" He takes her hands between both of his, rubs them and blows on them. *Oh no. Nathan is blowing on my hands.*

"No." She gently pulls her hands away.

"Just so you know," Nathan says, "I saw people in the parking lot with surveillance equipment and stuff."

"The police?"

"Not the police. They were wearing camouflage outfits."

"Do you think they'll find me?"

"They would find you here. You should go deeper in the woods. I'll help you find a spot."

Nathan sticks his hands in his pockets and looks at the stars. "If it was meteor season, my one wish would be that you come through this safe." He shifts from one foot to the other. Dani wonders why he isn't directing her to the new spot and why he isn't leaving.

"Tell me where it is and I'll go on my own. I don't want you taking risks for me." She begins gathering her blanket and other belongings.

"Please don't send me away just yet, Dani. I want to sit a few minutes and talk like we used to before rehearsal."

"You would only get yourself in trouble staying here."

"But I want to have an unending conversation with you," Nathan says. "That's part of my reason for coming here."

"What does 'an unending conversation' mean?"

"Where every day we talk about the things we discussed the day before, and we see if either of us has anything to add."

"Nathan, is this food and stuff really from the Hawtones? Or just from you?"

"I wouldn't use the phrase 'just me.'" He pauses. "It seems like you want me to go. But tell me if there's anything else you need."

"I don't have a phone. Can you please get a message to my mother and tell her I'm all right, too? And tell me how Gordy's taking it."

"I thought you might ask about him," Nathan says.

Nathan rests his hands on the small of his back, an old-mannish gesture, and breathes a sigh that makes his whole body shake. "This is the worst day of my life and the best. The worst because I've discovered that you care for someone else, and the best because I'm saving your life." He describes a group of boulders out of reach of the hiking trails that would make a good hiding place. He wants to carry her stuff, but Dani says no. She'll go alone, and the thoughts will follow her deeper into the woods, just as they followed her here.

"One more thing," Dani says, testing her flashlight under cover of her hand. "I almost hate to ask you."

"Go ahead, Dani. Anything."

"Go past the Drapers' house at 16 Dell Place. A boy named Alex lives there. Try to see if he's all right. I worry about him all the time."

86

Protect Our Kids
Chat Room

SHEEPDOGG: What will you do with her when you find her?

ROWDIE: Mileage may vary.

SHEEPDOGG: Meaning?

ROWDIE: We make the punishment fit the crime. First we have a tribunal where we read the accusations and weigh the evidence. Then our executive committee decides what should be done. Many of the people we apprehend are permanently removed from society, others are held for a period of time in our compound (I can't tell you where it is), and some are . . . changed in various ways so that they can never commit that particular crime again.

SHEEPDOGG: Changed in what way? Physically? Do you mean like rehabilitated?

ROWDIE: Depends. Various ways.

Wow, Malcolm thinks. *This is serious. I'm taking on a lot of responsibility here.* He's a little scared, but he gives himself a mental high-five.

SHEEPDOGG: Once all the evidence is read and whatnot, is the person ever just let go?

ROWDIE: Almost never.

SHEEPDOGG: Sounds like a well-oiled operation.

ROWDIE: We think so. Have a good day in school tomorrow, kid.

87

Lights flash in the distance. Dani hears a helicopter overhead. Every sound suggests that the people Nathan saw are about to find her. She lies awake in the new spot, but she'll need some sleep in order to be clearheaded tomorrow. Maybe each night she'll move to a different hiding place.

She remembers telling Alex the night world wasn't scary.

"We're going to bed now," Dani said, "but not everyone is. Some people are staying up. They'll be in charge while we rest."

"Which people?" Alex asked.

She showed him the harbor lights from the bedroom. "The fishermen out there and the police and the firefighters and the ambulance drivers and everyone at the hospital."

"Like Mom."

"Your mom and the other doctors and nurses. And the people in the twenty-four-hour pharmacy."

"Walgreen's?"

"Walgreen's and Denny's and the convenience store and the rest stop on the highway. And truck drivers."

Dani left the hall light on for Alex and didn't go back for the rest of the night. That was before the thoughts.

88

Channel 5

MetroBoston Eleven o'Clock News

Reporter: I'm Selda Binney and we're live from Hawthorne, Massachusetts, where a community still reels from the local newspaper's revelation that a trusted babysitter is in fact a potential child murderer. I'm standing in front of Havenswood, a three-thousand-acre forest in the heart of Hawthorne, where babysitter Dani Solomon is believed to be bunkered.

Anchor: Selda, what are police saying about the babysitter's whereabouts and actions?

Reporter: The police have chosen not to participate in the search, Lakshmi. Stepping into the breach is a grassroots organization called Protect Our Kids.

Anchor: And what level of threat does she pose to the public?

Reporter: It's important for our viewers to know that a criminal who is cornered is at his or her most desperate and dangerous. However, where Dani Solomon is concerned, it's believed that her particular pathology causes her to focus only on children. If you see a girl matching this photo, be sure not to leave your children alone. Sources believe that Solomon might arm herself with a knife.

Anchor: Thank you, Selda. To be honest, I love my job, but I don't know how you place yourself in harm's way day in and day out. On behalf of all of us at Channel 5, I just want to say, please . . . be careful out there in Havenswood.

89

"I'm sort of tempted, Dad," Malcolm says.

"Tempted by what?" his father asks.

"To go run around in the woods with the camouflage people. I think it would be a hoot."

"Oh God. You stay away from that crowd, Malky," Michael says. "They look like a bunch of whack jobs."

90

"I think Gordy is so cute," Meghan says. "In fact, I think he's one of the hottest guys in the school. What do you think, Shell?"

"There's nothing wrong with him," Shelley says. This is awkward. It might not be so bad except that they're in the music room and Gordy stands beside them in the circle, waiting for rehearsal to start.

"Well, if not Gordy, then who is? Who do you think is the hottest guy in school?"

"Cut it out, Meghan," Shelley says. "I don't necessarily think in superlatives."

"You're going to tell me you've never noticed this guy? You've never noticed how hot he is?" Meghan grabs Gordy around the waist and rests her chin on his shoulder.

"It's all right, Shelley," Gordy says, extracting himself from Meghan's arms. "That's enough, Meg. I'm not a politician or a rock star. I don't need to be universally loved."

"Who would you pick, if not Gordon?" Meghan asks, pressing her head next to Gordy's.

Pick someone else. You have to pick someone. Shelley feels her face burn in confusion.

"Of course Gordon is cute," Shelley says. "He's adorable."

"All right, then," Gordy says. He pushes Meghan off him gently. "There you have it."

"And you know what his best feature is?" Shelley continues.

"What? He's so cute, how could anyone choose just one?" Meghan asks. Gabler is in the room now. It's one of their last rehearsals.

"His lips. Dani always said he had these well-developed lips from playing the horn."

"She said that?" Gordy asks, looking at her sideways while he organizes his music.

"She always said that," Shelley replies. "Even before you guys were dating."

"Sweet," Gordon says, smiling.

91

Shelley describes her situation to her friends in the chat room Global Youth:

> "I really like this girl. I don't know if she's gay or straight or bi or what. She seems to like me too . . . sometimes she even seems to be pursuing me . . . but then she also flirts with boys."
>
> "Let her go she merely toys with you," says someone from Denmark.
>
> "Sounds a little manipulative," says someone from South Africa.
>
> "ENJOY HER—ENJOY IT—THEN MOVE ON. HOW OLD ARE YOU, ANYWAY? LIVE A LITTLE AND DON'T BE SUCH A SAD FACE," says someone from Montreal.

If only Dani were here to bounce this off of, Shelley thinks, logging off for the night. *Dani. Oh, Dani, I'm in over my head.*

92

A hand strokes Dani's hair. She wakes up and shines her flashlight in the intruder's face.

"God, I'm sorry," Gordy says, shielding his eyes. "I freaked you out."

Dani turns off the flashlight. "This is surreal," she says.

Seeing Gordy now is like being on a class field trip when she was little. She didn't believe all those other kids existed outside of her classroom. She didn't know Gordy existed in the middle of the night.

"Nathan told me where to find you," Gordy says. "Do you mind that I'm here? You told me to stay away, but I thought I could help. I don't want to seem like a stalker."

"Don't be silly. You're not a stalker." She sits up and makes a space beside her, but Gordy remains standing.

"I can sneak you out right now. I've been checking the parking lot every hour. It's two a.m. and all the cars and trucks are gone. The searchers or rescuers or whoever they are must be resting. I hid my truck behind an abandoned house on the side road. If we go now and stay close to that edge of the woods, no one will see us. This is the time to leave. We have to start walking now, before it gets light and the cars come back."

"I'm not leaving," Dani says, pulling the blanket around her.

"You're not? But it's been a couple of nights already. How long do you think you can stay here?"

She takes a deep breath. "As long as I can survive. I have to figure out a way to live here. I can't return to Hawthorne. I came here by accident, but I've decided I'm better off."

Gordy stares at her a minute before speaking. "Excuse me for saying this, but that's kind of ridiculous."

"If I go back, I might hurt someone," Dani says, as clearly as possible.

"Like that little kid?" he asks. His voice softens.

"Yes." *He doesn't disbelieve it anymore. He knows I'm crazy. Just like everyone in Hawthorne knows.*

Gordy moves closer, no longer so eager to be on the move. "It seems like you did the right thing by quitting babysitting. You really liked that kid, didn't you?"

"I guess I would say I loved him."

"That must have been rough. Will you tell me what it was like?"

Dani slides over some more so Gordy can sit beside her. "I got these thoughts, and I didn't want to have them. And the harder I tried to get rid of them, the more I had."

"I know what you mean," Gordy says. His smile seems inappropriate.

"You do?" Dani asks.

"Yes. I've been trying not to think of you since you told me to go away, but the more I tried, the more you were on my mind. I think I'm falling in love with you. Is that all right?"

"It's all right," Dani echoes. She thinks again how bad the timing is. If this was six months ago, she'd be overjoyed. "I was in love with you, too, even before we knew each other."

I could kill Gordon. I could bury his body out here and no one would find it.

"Was? You're not in love with me now?"

"I have to put it on hold. There are too many problems."

Gordy pulls leaves from Dani's hair. "Dani, tell me what you're thinking right now. Go ahead and tell me. I don't care how nasty it is."

She watches his face, knowing what the response will be. "I'm thinking I could kill you. I could bury your body out here and no one would find it."

Gordon's face pulls back and his eyebrows shoot up. "You think about hurting me, too?"

People always look that way when they hear her thoughts. Like they've been shot in the face with an air rifle.

"Whew," Gordy says. He gets to his feet.

"You're going back to your car, aren't you?" Dani says. A spider walks across her thigh, but she doesn't care. "Now that you know."

"Actually, no," Gordy says, grabbing the small pack he brought with him. "Remember when I said that I don't care if I end up getting hurt? When I say something like that, I generally mean it. I'm going to patrol the perimeter and make sure you're still safe."

Dani lies back and closes her eyes. In a few minutes Gordy returns. He stands over her, drinking from a Boy Scout canteen.

"Dani," he says, more emphatically this time. "Do you know what I used to say to myself when I saw you on the tennis court?"

"What?"

"Man, that girl isn't afraid of anything."

"Nice pep talk," Dani says. The answer seems obvious. She can't get away from what she's afraid of, because she's afraid of herself.

"Look, I've discussed it with my dad. You can stay at our house if you want. He'll get you a bodyguard, or a doctor or a lawyer or anything else you need. We have a place in Maine, too. You can stay there if you want to get away."

Gordy is lingering too long. Dani doesn't care if the camouflage people find her, but she doesn't want them to find Gordy. "You should get out now," she tells him. "You're too nice a guy to get messed up in this."

Gordy doesn't appear to listen. He sits on a nearby granite ledge for a long, quiet moment. He studies the stars, the way Nathan did. Dani is already sick of the stars.

"Did you know your mother was on TV?" Gordy says finally, without looking at her.

"She was?" Mom on TV. How truly strange life was becoming.

"She was begging you to come home."

"I didn't know that," Dani says.

"She looked like the living dead. There's more than one way to hurt someone, you know."

Dani gets up. She squeezes her hands together, thinking about her mother's distress. She shakes the blanket and starts stuffing it into one of the grocery bags.

"You'll come with me, then?" Gordy asks.

"Yes."

"You should leave all this," he suggests.

"Why?"

"To throw them off track. Let's make it look like you plan to stay another night. Keep them busy while we get you out of here."

93

National Envestigator News Online

SICKO SITTER SMILED WHEN FESSING KILL THOUGHTS

"Made My Skin Crawl," Declares Tot's Mom

94

"Put me in, Coach," Dani says to Gordy as they arrive at her house before sunrise. She's been hiding on the floor of the Lexus while Gordy drove back to town.

"I feel really rude not coming in to meet your mom," Gordy says. "Is that stupid?"

"She'd love to meet you. But this isn't the time."

"Good luck," Gordy says, watching the rearview mirror in case the camouflage people have seen them. Dani climbs over the pool fence. She crosses the patio. On the back door is a sign:

NO PRESS

NO GAWKING

NO KIDDING

TRESPASSERS WILL BE PROSECUTED

A new, heavier door covers their old screen door. Dani bangs. Sean opens the door.

"Beth," he says, staring at Dani with a stony face. "Your daughter is home."

"Dani!" Beth screams, coming up behind him. "You made it home!" In the kitchen, Beth presses into Dani so forcefully, Dani feels like she might become part of her. She cries so hard that it's a minute before she can talk. "I thought I might never see you again. My God, you look so filthy! Your friend from the music group told me you were all right."

"Nathan," Dani says. "I hid in the woods. He helped me."

"I went into the woods myself to look for you. Did anyone touch you, Dani? Did anyone hurt you? I can take you to the hospital. You might be dehydrated."

"No one hurt me. I got out in time. I need food and a bath and a bed, but I don't think I should stay."

"We'll take care of you, Dani. Sean and I will. But you're right. You're not staying."

95

The Dogg House

Sniffing Out That Babysitter

Your blog host: Sheepdogg

She's *Ba-a-ack*!

There's no place like home for Miss Mayhem the Blade Babe.

Increased activity around the heavily vandalized home suggests that this predator has returned to the nest. BetSo made a rare trip to the town shopping center for provisions, and a delivery was made from DD's favorite Thai restaurant. Who will be first to welcome her home? Just watch out for the big rent-a-cop stationed in the driveway.

96

After Dani takes a shower and a nap, she goes into the living room. A sheet of plywood covers the plate-glass window, which has been replaced. The curtains on all the other windows are closed, so the lights are on even though it's morning.

Beth's laptop is open on the coffee table. The inbox is loaded with e-mails that have threats right in the subject line. Beth shows Dani a message that she has saved. The sender is named MMandel. The message is only one line: "I think I can help your daughter."

"You're going to Boston for a while," Beth says.

"By myself?"

"Sean is taking you this afternoon. I'll join you later. Now come into the bathroom."

Beth ignores Dani's questions and sets her on the toilet lid. She takes a pair of long scissors from the cabinet and starts chopping off big sections of Dani's damp hair.

"I don't know how to cut hair. I've never done it before. I need to wrap some things up here, then I'll come stay with you. You're getting your phone back and I want you to call me every hour on the hour to let me know you're all right. Oh my God. This looks awful. I have no idea how to do this." She starts crying again.

Sean stands awkwardly in the doorway of the bathroom.

"Why don't we call a professional hairdresser, Beth? Lots of them will come to the house."

"I don't care how I look," says Dani. "I just want to get out of town."

"I want to do it," Beth says. "I'm doing it. Go away, Sean. Just go away for an hour and leave us alone."

"Where will I stay in Boston?" Dani asks, flinching from her mother's ravaging hands.

"In a hotel. We'll be there together."

"For how long?"

"I don't know yet."

Beth opens a box and mixes one bottle with another. She pours the stuff over Dani's head. It runs onto a towel around Dani's shoulders.

"We'll have to toss this T-shirt," Beth says. "I'm not being very careful right now." Her hands move roughly on Dani's scalp, lathering the dye into her hair.

97

Beth believes people have been following her car, so she doesn't want Dani to ride in it. She arranges for Sean to take Dani into Boston in a borrowed truck marked NORTH SHORE LANDSCAPING. The rent-a-cop sits in the passenger seat. Sitting in the back of the truck doesn't feel much friendlier than the day the cops drove Dani home. Dani doesn't feel like spending ten minutes with Sean. He acts okay when Beth is around, like he's putting up with Dani. But when they're alone, resentment radiates off him. She bets he wishes she hadn't come back from the woods.

"I hope you know what you're putting your mom through," he says after paying the toll at the Tobin Bridge. "How do you think she can hold her head up with all the people she has to meet? What kinds of things do you think they're saying?"

"I'm really sorry about Mom," Dani says, making clear that her apology is limited to Beth. Although Sean acts mournful, Dani believes he's glad he has more reasons to take a side against her.

"So this is where you two will stay," he says, pointing to a narrow brick building. Only a small brass plaque by the door identifies it as a hotel. He drives a few more blocks and stops at a brownstone on Commonwealth Avenue. "And this is where your mother thinks you'll get better."

part 5 INSIDE OUT

98

Hawthorne *Beacon-Times*

PD: SOLOMON "GONE"

Dani Solomon has left Hawthorne for an unspecified period to receive intensive psychological treatment, the *Beacon-Times* has learned. A spokesman for the Hawthorne Police confirmed that the troubled teen has moved to an undisclosed location after surviving for several days in Havenswood. Public information officer Sergeant Philip Mason emphasized that Solomon is undergoing treatment voluntarily and is not wanted for any crime. "There is no crime, there is no case, and we wish her the best," Mason stated. "Case closed."

99

Rowdie wrote:

You see, Dogg, she slipped away. Once again, local law enforcement exposed as ineffectual pantywaists.

100

Malcolm goes to the back porch to help his father stare at the yard. His father used to drink a lot of beer and rant and rave. Now he drinks soda and simmers quietly.

101

Protect Our Kids

Member Alerts

New message from: Rowdie

Protect our kids by determining where potential kiddie killer Dani Solomon has been institutionalized and for how long. This is the time to activate any contacts with hospital employees. Not just doctors, nurses, health aides, and technicians but security, food service, and maintenance workers. Distribute photo of Dani Solomon to everyone you know in the health industry, especially hospitals with big psych units such as McLean and Mass General. Offer cash reward if need be. Send any and all leads to operative Sheepdogg.

POK over police

We care about community.

102

"Tell me about these intrusive thoughts."

Dr. Mandel is a petite, white-blond woman in a brown leather armchair. She wants Dani to call her Mathilde, but her European accent makes her seem inaccessible, as if to call her by her first name would mean crossing an entire ocean.

"They're kind of embarrassing. I mean, I'm ashamed of them."

"Just tell me. Say them. Whether they're embarrassing or not."

"Some of them are so weird and ridiculous."

"Go ahead."

Dani tells Dr. Mandel her thoughts about stabbing Alex, yelling homophobic remarks to Shelley, grabbing Mr. Gabler's testicles, knocking her mother off the ladder and calling her a dried-up twat, cutting Gordy to pieces, and leaving Nathan's body in the woods.

"Are there any others?" Dr. Mandel asks.

Dani describes her fear of telling the neighbors that they're going to die soon and hitting Mrs. Alex with a tennis racket.

"I know you've just met me, but do you think I'm going to do any of those things?" Dani asks. She pulls her striped dress down to cover her knees. Beth packed her a bag with good dresses and sandals, a Coach purse, even lip gloss. Dr. Mandel's office is so fancy that Dani's glad she dressed up.

"I don't know. Nothing is a hundred percent sure in life, is it?"

Dani is disappointed. She had hoped that Dr. Mandel would tell her the thoughts were ridiculous and that she was a nice, caring person who would never hurt anyone.

"So I might really do those things I thought about?"

"There's a chance that you might. I'm not in the business of giving reassurance."

"Does that mean that you're afraid of me?"

"No," says Dr. Mandel. "Let me ask you another question. When you had upsetting thoughts, what did you do?"

Dani doesn't understand. "Not enough, I guess, because I tried to make the thoughts go away, but I couldn't."

"Did you have any routines or rituals?"

"No."

"Was there anything you would regularly do to try to make yourself feel better?"

"I don't think so."

"What did you do to avoid performing these acts you had thought about?"

"Oh, yeah"—Dani laughs, because it seems strange to tell someone this—"I asked my mother to lock her door so I wouldn't kill her. I also took some of the knives out of Mrs. Alex's kitchen and hid them in the garage so I couldn't get at them."

"Dani, have you heard of obsessive-compulsive disorder?"

"I don't have that," Dani says.

"Why do you say that?"

"Because a girl in my school, a senior, had OCD and she

was missing classes because she was in the bathroom constantly, washing her hands. Her hands got all red and cracked. Her name was Layla Amundsen, but people called her Lobster Claw. Not to her face, though, because she was mostly normal and actually kind of popular. She was really open about what she had. When she started to get better, she talked about it at Health Day. She even did a display about OCD at the science fair. I don't see what that has to do with my having bad thoughts."

"That's because you have a different type. Some people worry about getting sick, so they always wash their hands. You worry about hurting people, so you hide knives.

"You have obsessions—thoughts that wouldn't go away—followed by compulsions—activities you have to do in order to feel better."

Dani never looked at her problems this way, as a thought followed by an action. She's surprised that Dr. Mandel can place her problems in a pattern.

"Are you saying that you've met other people who think the same way?" she asks.

"Many."

Dani looks down at her hands, folded in her lap. They're strong and soft with shiny oval nails, but she wishes they were the cracked and scaly mitts of Lobster Claw.

"You look sad right now, Dani."

"I'm envious of Layla."

"Why?"

"Because she could be open about her OCD, but I can't be open about what I have."

"Why not?"

Dani unfolds her hands and smooths her skirt again. "Because what I have scares people."

Dr. Mandel leans forward. "There's no one at all that you can be open with?"

"My mom," Dani says. "And this guy I've been dating." She thinks for a minute. "And . . . I have a friend. We got on the wrong track. But when I get better I'd like to tell her everything."

"It sounds like you're looking forward to getting better. What else do you need to know about this illness?"

"I don't understand why the thoughts change so much. I begin to expect certain ones, but then new ones pop up in different situations when I totally don't expect them. I can't keep up. It's driving me crazy."

Dr. Mandel nods, as if she's heard this before. "The nature of the thoughts is that they can change to suit the thinker and the setting. They mutate into whatever you would find most repugnant."

"So the thoughts are happening on their own? I'm not really going to do those things? I'm not really a potential murderer?"

"I don't know. There are murderers in many populations. Some of them may have OCD."

"Please, tell me I'm not going to kill anyone. I won't even need any more treatment if you tell me that. That will be the end of it. Just tell me I'm not a murderer and I'll go away happy."

"I can't, Dani. I'm sorry if it sounds cold, but the way the therapy works is that I can't reassure you. You have to live with the anxiety that your worst nightmares may come true. That's the chance you have to take in order to get better."

Dr. Mandel asks Dani to rank her thoughts from least upsetting to most upsetting.

"That's easy," Dani decides after a while. The more damage she could cause, the more distressing the thought is to her. So thoughts about hurting or killing bother her more than thoughts of shocking people or yelling insults, even though those actions could have lasting effects, like getting suspended or losing someone's friendship.

"You look sad again," Dr. Mandel says.

Dani squeezes her hands together. "A lot of damage has already been done. Even though I haven't killed or insulted anyone. When I go back, my life won't be the same."

"Can you undo any of the damage?"

"If people let me I can."

"What is that you're doing with your hands?" Dr. Mandel asks.

"When I think about hurting another person I do this to make sure I'm not really touching anyone."

"Does it help?"

"Only for a minute."

"Then maybe it's time to try something that works better."

103

Dani's mother waits in a rented car outside Dr. Mandel's, dressed in business clothes. Dani hasn't seen her since the morning.

"We're back to looking alike!" Beth says.

"Not bad," Dani replies. Her mother has dyed her hair black.

Both of them wear sunglasses. Beth takes her to the Thai restaurant on the first floor of their hotel and requests a corner table close to the door.

"So how was your first day?" Beth asks.

"Sort of surprising. Dr. Mandel seems very familiar with what I have."

"That's a relief."

"I know. That part made me feel much better. But when I asked her if she thought I would actually kill someone, she said that was a possibility."

Beth gets that airgun look again. "Well . . . ," she begins. "To be honest, I thought about taking you to a facility that was more . . ."

"More what?"

"More of an inpatient facility. Someplace secure." Dani rubs her hands. Her mother means a place where she would be locked up. That sounds appealing, actually, like the woods. A place where she couldn't hurt anyone. "But Dr. Mandel said she didn't think it was necessary," Beth finishes.

"I guess she must know," Dani says uncertainly.

"Anyway, here's to your recovery," Beth toasts Dani with a Diet Coke. They eat quickly and return to their suite. It has two bedrooms and a sitting room. Beth locks the door to her bedroom.

104

The Dogg House

Sniffing Out That Babysitter

Your blog host: Sheepdogg

Where There's Death, There's Beth?

Beth Solomon's car has been parked in the driveway 24/7 (not her style at all—hmmm), but from the looks of it BetSo has not been sleeping at home. Most likely the Predator's Parent is doing the mother-hen thing at whatever institution Deadly Daughter is checking out, and we're not talking about college visits here. Boston? Belmont? Newton? Dogg suspects they've hightailed it to Aspen, Colorado, where the right money can hush up a private nuthouse.

In the meantime, the spoiled son of a rich lawyer in town is looking pretty mopey, and the sicko's sidekick is sobbing on a certain same-sex shoulder. It's not exactly *Girls Gone Wild*, but if the sight of four tanned legs and four perky breasts united in budding more-than-friendship turns you on, you may want to check it out.

"How are they getting all this information?" Dani asks Beth. "They don't even know me."

"Stop reading that stuff," Beth says. "Stop looking at that stuff and just ignore them."

105

Channel 5 News

Consumer Corner

Anchor: Parents are asking, How do I know if my babysitter is safe? Now a New Bedford high-tech company specializing in surveillance equipment is helping parents in crisis. Call it . . . the babysitter trap. Michael Soares of HomeSpy Technologies has developed a fascinating tool for keeping our loved ones secure. Michael?

Guest: Meredith, HomeSpy has created a brand-new product called the Dani Cam for parents who want to keep their kids safe.

Anchor: How does it work, Michael?

Guest: The Dani Cam is more than just a hidden surveillance camera. It's a proprietary, fully customizable suite of cameras, sensors, and computers. It uses state-of-the-art image processing technology to recognize you, your children, and the babysitter. When either a child or the babysitter behaves in a way that's out of the ordinary, it will send an alarm to both the police and your cell phone.

Anchor: What red flags trigger an alarm?

Guest: On the babysitter's part, the presence of a gun or knife, or violent behavior such as striking, shaking, or strangling. We also provide these wired T-shirts for your kids to wear anytime the babysitter is in the house. The shirts alert you to any abnormal physical signs such as slowed breathing or a decrease in body temperature. Of course, the system isn't going to wait for a red flag before it starts talking to you. It learns all your daily routines and will signal when the child has been put to bed too late or too early or if the babysitter has brought unauthorized friends or visitors into the home. The Dani Cam is unquestionably the next generation in protection against your babysitter.

Anchor: Sounds like just what parents need in these uncertain times.

Guest: That's the world we live in, Meredith.

106

Dani turns off the television. She pokes around the *Beacon-Times* site to see what's been going on at school. She reads the 177 comments on the article "Solomon 'Gone,'" including this one:

> Rowdie wrote:
> Do not allow the constraints of "law" to tie your hands when it comes to your children's safety.

Rowdie has posted a link to the POK website, and Dani follows it.

107

On the POK website are photos of people accused of crimes against children. Each person holds a sign saying PROTECT OUR KIDS. Across each photo is the word *Exterminated*, *Detained*, or *Modified*. Another group of pictures is labeled *At Large*. Her tennis photo from the *Beacon-Times* is one of them. Each page of the site has a PayPal widget so people can give donations. When she shows Beth the website, Beth calls their lawyer to try to have the photo removed.

Dani texts Gordy:

"It's good to be out of Hawthorne. Thanks for helping me. Miss you. Still can't tell you where I am."

Gordy replies:

"As long as I know you're safe."

108

Shelley finds a note in her locker:

"I'm really glad we're hanging out together. A lot of bad stuff has happened lately. But without the bad stuff happening, some of the good stuff would not have happened, like us getting to be such good friends."

Hanging from the coat hook is a soft, pale blue bear with a ribbon around his neck.

Shelley thinks, *It's just like my parents always say. When God closes a door, He opens a window.*

109

"Let's talk some more about Alex," Dr. Mandel suggests.

Dani clasps her hands.

"What kinds of thoughts did you have about Alex?"

"I don't like talking about it. He's only a little kid. I hate talking about what happened with him."

"I know, but you've been doing so well."

Dani tells the doctor about how trusting Alex is, how much he looks up to her, how sometimes he even said that he liked her more than his own mother. She tells about the thoughts of going up to his room with a knife and parts of him that should be inside showing on the outside. But the worst part is the look in his eyes when he sees her, when the bad stuff is about to happen, and how he realizes that she is not the person he thought she was. Sometimes she imagined waking him up first, and telling him, "I'm going to kill you." She also imagined Alex saying something he would never say because he's so little and it would all be moving so fast, but she can't get the phrase out of her mind. It's like what Shelley said when she figured out that Dani was the babysitter: "You, Dani, you?"

"How do you feel right now, talking about Alex?"

"My heart is pounding and my palms feel tingly."

"That's to be expected."

Beth meets Dani outside after the session. Dani is so rattled that she's silent all the way to the hotel.

110

Shelley fantasizes about inviting Meghan to the end-of-season tennis banquet so that everyone will know they're together and Meghan can see how important Shelley is to the team and watch her get announced as a co-captain for her senior year. But Shelley could never do that. She knows people do it at some schools. But not here.

111

"A couple of days ago we ranked your thoughts," Dr. Mandel says. "Do you remember that?"

"Yes," Dani says. "I told you I was more upset about thoughts of killing someone than insulting them."

"Let's start with the insults then," Dr. Mandel says, "and work our way up to the more upsetting thoughts. I'm not going to try to make you stop thinking these things. That would be like asking you not to think of an orange sea lion—all you'd be able to think about would be orange sea lions. Instead I'll help you expose yourself to the thoughts without seeking relief in your compulsions. Eventually, the thoughts will become less disturbing. Only by accepting the thoughts, not fighting them, can you cause them not to have power over you."

Dr. Mandel has Dani visualize and describe, in great detail, what it would be like to call her mother a dried-up twat: the ugly word bursting out of Dani's mouth, her mother's face crumpled in hurt and disbelief, Dani's knowledge that her mother is vulnerable because her father left Beth for a younger woman, and because her mother feels insecure about how desirable she is to her stupid boyfriend. Dani wants to touch her mouth to make sure she hasn't said *twat* to her mother. But she folds her hands in her lap.

Next Dr. Mandel has Dani imagine outing Shelley, calling her a dyke in front of the Monsignor Deagle tennis team: Shelley's humiliation; the surprise of the other team, which expects Dani to be the epitome of good sportsmanship; the shock of her coaches; the anger of everyone in the Gay-Straight Alliance and maybe even the school administration once the incident is reported. Worst of all, Dani is revealed as an unworthy friend.

"How do you feel?" Dr. Mandel asks at the end of the hour.

"Awful," Dani tells her. "It seems like if I can imagine those things, I'm just one step away from them coming true. But actually, the words are bothering me a little less than they did an hour ago."

"Good. See you tomorrow," Dr. Mandel says.

112

Every time Shelley looks at the blue bear she feels a little braver. On her run after school she wonders if it's time to tell Meghan about her feelings. In the coming-out stories she read on the Internet or heard at GSA, people discussed the best way to tell someone you like them as more than a friend. Some lucky people were out from age twelve or thirteen. But what if, like Shelley, you were not openly gay? Should you come out to that person and wait for a reaction, or should you skip that part and tell the person about your feelings? The safest way is to start by saying that you're gay. If you're really lucky, the other person will say "me too."

Shelley keeps thinking about it as she cools down a block from the house. She doesn't want to decide too soon. She's never said "I love you" to anyone but family and friends. She's never kissed or held hands with a girl, only with boys, and there was nothing exciting about it. *I want to hurry, but I don't want to*, Shelley thinks, going home to babysit for her brother, Ralphie. *I want this part of my time with Meghan to last forever.*

113

"What will we work on today?" Dani asks Dr. Mandel when she returns to the office.

"Let's hear about the insults to Shelley and your mom," says Dr. Mandel.

"Again?"

Dani imagines a tennis match in which she goes up to the linesman and announces Shelley's gayness over a loudspeaker. She imagines calling her mother a dried-up twat, but this time she says it in front of Sean. Dani feels even more anxious than when she started therapy.

"What will we work on tomorrow?" Dani asks.

"The same thing," Dr. Mandel replies.

114

By the fifth day Dani has become accustomed to the anxiety the words *dyke* and *twat* create. She's anxious, but a little bored at the same time.

"Can we move on to something else?" she asks.

"Let's give it one more day," Dr. Mandel insists.

115

Meghan tells Shelley about the boyfriend she had back in Pennsylvania, where she lived until two years ago. "Sam and I met in a coffeehouse," she says. "He's a really great singer/songwriter and he wrote some songs for me. He sent me one recently, as a matter of fact."

"Cool. How come you guys broke up?" Shelley asks.

"Because I moved here."

Maybe Meghan is using the old boyfriend as a cover, as a beard. Shelley has referred to boys as boyfriends too, but those boys never meant anything. Shelley wishes Dani were here to hear, study, and analyze every word Meghan says. It's tough going through something like this alone.

116

"How is your anxiety today, Dani?" Dr. Mandel asks.

"Not bad."

"Can you assign it a number from one to ten?"

"Somewhere between four and six."

Dani is tired of being cooped up in the hotel so much of the time. Yesterday she went to a bookstore with Beth's credit card. She bought a Jane Austen novel, two movies, and some workout DVDs they could do together in the room. And Beth let her jog around the neighborhood wearing large sunglasses and a hat. No one seemed to have been following her. She hopes that in a day or two Beth will loosen up enough that the two of them can go to some concerts and museums.

"Let's try to raise your anxiety a bit. Tell me more about the knives in Alex's house that bothered you. The ones you moved to the garage. What did they look like? How large were they?"

"The one that weirded me out was pretty large, the kind you would use to carve roast beef." Dani rubs her hands together.

"How is your anxiety level now?" Dr. Mandel removes her glasses to wipe them.

"Climbing. Maybe an eight?"

Dr. Mandel reaches into her desk and takes out a carving knife.

"Was the largest knife something like this?" she says, holding it with the point up.

"Very much like that," Dani says. *Oh my God*, she thinks.

"How is your anxiety now?"

"Definitely a ten. You surprised me." In the last few sessions, Dani had to vividly describe the ways she might kill Nathan, Gordy, and her mother. But she did not expect to see a knife in Dr. Mandel's office, and she doesn't know where the doctor got it from. For a second she believes that this is the actual knife from Alex's house, that it has been brought here as evidence to prove something about her. She's afraid of what she might do.

"Remember," the doctor says, "I don't want you to fight the thoughts. I want you acknowledge them and grow accustomed to the anxiety."

"Is that knife from Alex's house?"

"It may be."

"How did you get it? Why is it here?"

"Remember not to rub your hands. How is your anxiety?"

"Through the roof," Dani says. "Beyond ten."

"Come stand by my desk." Dr. Mandel sounds like a teacher on the first day of school.

Dr. Mandel unties her checked silk scarf.

"Hold the knife up to my throat," she says. "But don't touch me."

"I don't want to," she says.

"I want you to," Dr. Mandel says firmly.

Dani folds her hands behind her back.

"Unclasp your hands. Take the knife. It's the only way you'll get better."

"But how can you be sure I won't kill you?" Dani asks, holding the heavy knife. She feels sick. For months she's thought how a knife like this would feel. That doesn't mean she wants to feel it.

"I can't be sure," Dr. Mandel says, unbuttoning the top button of her white blouse. "Do you know where the arteries are?"

"There's one on either side."

"Maybe that would be a good spot."

"How do you know I won't kill you?" Dani asks again.

Dr. Mandel sets her eyeglasses on the desk. She leans back like she's about to take a nap. As her head falls back, Dani sees and smells her neck: plump, white, unwrinkled, with a trace of fragrant body powder. "Maybe you will and maybe you won't," Dr. Mandel says.

Dani stands over the therapist. "You must trust me then," Dani says to Mathilde. "You must trust me a lot. That's what you're trying to tell me, right?"

"I can't reassure you. If it happens, it happens," Dr. Mandel says.

Dani examines the knife. She has never looked at a knife so carefully before. This one is nearly a foot long, with a wedge-shaped blade imprinted with L. L. HOENICHER ENDURO STAINLESS. The other side says JAPAN in tiny letters. Dani tilts the blade so it catches glints of light.

"Go ahead now," Dr. Mandel says.

Dani turns the edge of the knife toward Dr. Mandel's neck. The edge looks extremely sharp. *This must be a good knife*, she thinks. *Good enough to kill with.*

Dani could press the blade against Dr. Mandel's throat until she saw the skin shift. The line where the skin and the knife intersected would turn red, and that would be the last line to be crossed.

"Now say, 'I'm going to stab you, I'm going to kill you.'"

"I'm going to stab you. I'm going to kill you. Eleven! Eleven!" Dani says.

"Keep going," says Dr. Mandel.

Dani looks out at the other office buildings and the strip of park on Commonwealth Avenue, where people walk in a light summer rain with slickers, umbrellas, and dogs.

"I am going to stab you," Dani says. "I'm going to kill you.

"How long do I have to keep this up?" she asks. Her arm isn't getting tired exactly, but her hand is shaking a little and she's afraid something will go wrong.

"Just keep going," the doctor says. "You're doing great!"

Another five minutes. Dani's opportunity to kill Dr. Mandel is two-thirds over, yet a lot can happen in that last third. The side of the doctor's neck has a soft, jowly plumpness, and Dani could choose to slice it: for no reason, not even because she was crazy, but just to change things. She could pin the doctor's shoulder down so she can't move, then press the blade through the white plumpness. It would be as simple as making that first slice in the turkey on Thanksgiving. In the same way there are always second chances in life, there is always another chance to mess things up.

"Your anxiety level?" A puff of fragrance emanates from the doctor's throat.

"I'm having a lot of thoughts," Dani says. "Still eleven."

"Okay, you can put the knife down for today. You're doing very well, Dani. We'll try this again tomorrow."

117

Shelley goes to the tennis banquet without Meghan. Shelley's parents come to the banquet, as they do every year. Together they eat the food from the buffet. Shelley walks up during the awards to receive her trophy. She is named as next year's captain and gives a brief speech of thanks. There is no co-captain. Everyone tries to act like the Dani situation doesn't exist, because they want the banquet to be a nice event. Dani's name is on one of the trophies, but Mrs. Solomon is not there. After dessert it's as if a spell is broken and the nice part is officially over. The coach and Shelley's parents talk in low voices. The coach asks whether they saw any sign of Dani's problems, and whether Dani had been allowed to be around Shelley's little brother, Ralphie. Shelley thinks for a minute that she wishes she had mentioned Dani in her speech, because even if Dani is a horrible person, even if she is a child murderer, she's a good tennis player and she won those matches legitimately. She fought for every point.

While her parents are talking, Shelley texts Meghan:

"I was looking forward to this, but it isn't fun."

And Meghan writes back:

"Wish I could be there with you."

118

Dani goes to the *Beacon-Times* website. She looks at pictures of the end-of-year concert. Gordy had already told her Meghan got that solo, partly because Shelley lobbied for it. Pictures of the tennis banquet have begun to appear, of Shelley and the other top players holding their trophies for the camera. One trophy sits unclaimed behind them on the white-covered table.

119

Protect Our Kids
Chat Room
SHEEPDOGG: I didn't get any results from the last member alert. Who is your best operative in Aspen?
ROWDIE: Our members are losing interest in the case. It would have been different if she had actually killed someone. If there is no escalation, the story runs out of steam. I may close the dossier on this one. You done good, kid.
SHEEPDOGG: Let me know if you need me. Anywhere, anytime.
ROWDIE: You done good. You're a good kid.

120

In the morning Dani dresses in running clothes. She follows another runner to the Charles River, where she finds exercisers of all races, sizes, and ages but mostly college students and yuppies. She knows she blends in with them, that with her short, dyed hair even the most rabid tabloid photographer would have trouble recognizing her here. And in another year or two, if all goes well, she will be here for real, blending in. For now, she follows the flow of bikers and in-line skaters across lagoons and over footbridges, past the amphitheater and the tennis courts and the sailing pavilion. She follows two young women across the river to the Cambridge side, past the dome of MIT. She would worry about getting lost in the constantly shifting vistas except that everything is visible from the river, the skyscrapers and bridges and landmarks, and if you can't get back one way you can always get back another.

121

Malcolm has been spending too many hours on the news sites and the chat rooms. On his way home from school he thinks about—he savors—all the things he can do outdoors. He looks forward to doing some chores, working with his dad, and making his mom happy. His father likes the phrase "manicured lawn." Maybe today, Malcolm will create just that. He'll go around the edges of the yard with a nail scissor and trim every unruly blade of grass. How much would his mom brag then?

He stops at the convenience store and buys two fountain sodas.

"Where's Dad?" he says as he walks into the kitchen.

His mother is at the sink. "Out back," she snaps.

He drops his books on the table. "What's eating you?" he asks.

"I said he's out back."

"I got you a Mountain Dew with extra ice," he says when he finds his father on the patio.

"I'm all set," Michael says. On his knee is a bottle of Samuel Adams.

"Is that a beer, Dad?" Malcolm asks.

"No, it's a portrait of an important historical figure, and I just happen to like holding it in my hand."

All at once the yard seems too quiet. A butterfly lands on the butterfly bush Malcolm planted. Malcolm's dad hasn't had a drink since last summer. They were making this a little paradise.

"How long has this been going on?" Malcolm asks.

"A few days."

Malcolm looks back at the house. "Is that what's got Mom upset?"

His dad doesn't answer.

"I don't get it, Dad. Why?"

Michael Pinto holds up a newspaper he saved, with Dani's picture and the word *Monster*. "I guess I'm having trouble turning the page."

122

Shelley takes Meghan to the old handball court behind the school, where she will teach her to play tennis. She's surprised when Meghan doesn't seem to be athletic. Shelley assumed that all people with nicely toned bodies have good coordination.

"Tell me about your town in Pennsylvania," Shelley begins. It's a great time to talk because they're hitting side by side against the wall, not looking at each other.

"Hartswell. It's about a hundred fifty miles from Philadelphia. A lot of people were in dairy farming and just trying to make a living. My grandparents, for instance. Only a small core of people are interested in the arts or have any kind of ambition. Every day I dreamed of getting out of there. You wouldn't believe how excited I was when we moved here and I was going to be close to a big city, with concerts and Broadway-type shows and everything. But anyway, when I met Sam I thought I had met a kindred spirit because he was a musician."

Meghan swings at the air, then runs into the grass after the ball.

"I think you're turning your arm," Shelley says when Meghan gets back to her spot. "That's why you keep missing." She stops her own ball between her racket and her foot, then goes to Meghan's side. "Can I show you?"

"I think I'm getting it," Meghan says. "I just need to keep practicing."

Meghan's wearing a sports bra, weensy shorts, and a pair of unserious sneakers. Shelley stands behind her and grasps her arm. "Keep your elbow straight and hold this line right here. That way your racket can't turn parallel to the ground. Shift your weight to your front foot. Hey, your skin smells like grapefruit."

"That's my citrus body wash," Meghan says.

Shelley makes a decision. *I'm not going to ask her the exact name of the body wash. I'm not going to ask whether it's expensive and where she buys it. I'm not going to pretend that I want to imitate Meghan. I'm just going to leave my compliment out there.*

"It's nice," she says.

Meghan shrugs and moves away with a laugh. She starts hitting again, and the first few times she doesn't turn her arm.

"I was in Philadelphia once," Shelley says. "I was there on a family vacation to see the Liberty Bell and all that stuff. We sort of wandered into the wrong neighborhood, and there was a parade going on with a lot of same-sex couples. We saw two women holding hands. My parents pulled me away from there as soon as they could."

"That's gross," Meghan says, tossing the hair out of her eyes and getting ready to serve again.

Shelley stops playing. "I don't think it's gross. I think it's brave."

"You're entitled to your own opinion." Meghan keeps swatting at the ball.

Shelley's ball has stopped, but Shelley just stands there. "I can't believe you would say that. If you think two women holding hands is gross, why are you in the Gay-Straight Alliance?"

"Because I'm straight!" Meghan doesn't seem to know what Shelley is upset about. She taps the ball against the floor of the court. "It's a social group for gay people and straight people."

"But it's technically a support group for gay people, not a support group for straight people."

"It's open to everybody," Meghan says. "No group in the school is allowed to exclude anyone."

Shelley resumes hitting. She focuses everything she has on the bright green ball and hits without stopping, twenty times without a bounce and thirty-one times with a bounce before she breaks her rhythm. She wants to hide from Meghan right now, and if she keeps hitting like this she can pretend Meghan doesn't exist.

123

Shelley and Meghan walk halfway home together. Meghan chatters about how well the end-of-year concert went even though she forgot the words to "Old Cape Cod." Shelley wonders if Meghan truly believes nothing's wrong or if she's talking too much to cover up.

"Do you know about the singers' camp at Tanglewood, in the Berkshires?" Meghan asks. "You have to apply early, but they have these one-day master classes that usually have a few openings or cancellations."

Shelley shifts her tennis bag on her shoulder. She's carrying both rackets—her own and the one she brought for Meghan.

She wonders what Dani would have said about today. Would Dani have thought Meghan was right for her at all? Sometimes, when God closes a door, He opens a window. Then you jump out of it.

124

Malcolm dresses in a blue short-sleeved shirt, navy pants, and black shoes. It looks pretty close to a uniform. He combs his hair back carefully, which makes him look older. He prints a batch of business cards with the POK website and his cell number, but no name.

He goes to 16 Dell Place.

Cynthia Draper opens the door in shorts and a cotton blouse. His father was right; she's attractive for a woman with kids. "You're not a reporter, are you?" she says. "I'm not talking to reporters."

"No, ma'am. I don't want any information from you. I'm here to give you some information."

"What's that?"

"The group I'm with is an ALEA. Do you know what an ALEA is?"

"No, I don't," she says.

"It's an alternative law enforcement agency. As I said, I don't want any information. I just want you to know that in the eventuality that you ever have trouble with Dani Solomon again, we would be the best people to call."

Cynthia Draper is a cool customer. She looks at Malcolm and at the card without revealing either displeasure or relief. She takes the card and closes the door.

125

Dr. Mandel called Dani's hotel room and told her not to come up to the office. Instead they'll meet downstairs on the sidewalk.

Dani wonders what the doctor will do next. If Dr. Mandel's theories are valid, Dani has made progress over two weeks of intensive sessions. Yesterday she held the knife and was hardly bothered by anxiety. She sees the elevator open. Dr. Mandel strides out in a spring coat, with her purse over her arm.

"Come with me," says the doctor, turning Dani by the elbow onto Commonwealth Avenue. Mathilde is much shorter than Dani, but she motors along pretty well.

"Where are we going?"

"There are some experiences I can't give you on my own," says Dr. Mandel. "For that we need other people and another place."

"Is it far?" Dani asks.

"No, it's close." The scent of roses and honeysuckle reaches them from the long park in the center of the avenue. The air carries the creak of a swing set and the voices of children singing a Lady Gaga song. *You've got to be kidding me*, Dani thinks.

"Here we are," says Dr. Mandel. She opens the iron gate to a playground where a group of well-dressed three- and four-year-olds play while their mothers, fathers, and nannies sit on benches nearby. Some parents read the newspaper; others talk on their phones. None of them seem worried about their children. The parents and their kids feel at home here.

"Let's sit for a minute," the doctor suggests, bringing Dani to a bench. She nods to the woman and man beside them. The parents take stock of Dani and Mathilde and nod back.

"What a lovely spot," the doctor says to the others. "How's your anxiety?" she whispers to Dani.

"At least a nine," Dani says. "I can't quite get used to your surprises."

Although Boston is not far from Hawthorne, it seems a world away, like a cosmopolitan European capital. Dani could get used to the comfort of people not knowing her. She can't wait to come here for school and live on her own.

"Okay," says Dr. Mandel. She nods toward the kids. "Interact."

Dani walks to the swing set. Heads on the bench look up, take note of her, and resume what they were doing. Dani clasps her hands on her shoulder bag. She feels useless. It's not like the old days with Alex, who held on to her every second, told her she was his favorite person, and cajoled her into long games with incomprehensible rules and story lines. Alex was a job. She has no connection to these children. At least she'll make a good impression on the parents with her nice dress and sandals and best handbag. And she combed her hair with mousse so it looks smoother. People in the city are sharp and sophisticated. They notice those things.

"Will you push me?" asks a girl who has climbed onto the

swings. She has her hair in pigtails and wears board shorts in the pattern of an American flag.

Dani hikes her purse higher on her shoulder and helps the girl get settled. It's been a while since Dani's touched a child. She'd forgotten how really small they are.

"You can push me harder if you want," says the girl.

Dani puts her whole arm into the push.

"Hey, you're strong!" the girl calls to Dani over her shoulder.

The mother smiles at Dani before returning to her text message. "Luisa likes you," she says.

Dani thinks how easy it would be to knock Luisa off the swing by dope-slapping the back of her head. Or to stop the swing with one strong hand while the girl continued to fly. She imagines the mother's look of horror, this mother who just told Dani that Luisa liked her. Dani thinks of even worse things she could do, like wrapping the chain around the child's neck. Now, that was a weird one. That was really creative.

"Higher! Higher!" Luisa shouts, sensing Dani's distraction.

Dr. Mandel stands beside Dani. "How's your anxiety?" she asks.

"Nine," Dani says. "I keep coming up with new thoughts." But not all the thoughts are getting stuck. Some of them are moving: tacking and circling and passing like the sailboats she saw in the river.

126

That evening Shelley gets a ton of voice mails and text messages from Meghan.

"Why aren't you answering your phone?"

"Are you mad at me for something?"

"If it's our conversation on the handball court, I think you're overreacting."

Thank God I didn't go so far as to tell her my secret, Shelley thinks. *She was not the right person to tell my secret to.*

127

Watching TV with Ralphie that night, Shelley thinks about the time Dani tried to tell her her secret. Dani probably had other secrets to tell her too. Shelley was not the right person for Dani to tell. But she should have been, because she was supposed to be Dani's best friend.

128

"How is your anxiety?" Dr. Mandel asks at the playground three days later.

"Slightly better," Dani says. "Six or seven. The thoughts are there. I'm having them, but"—she gropes for the words—"I feel more at peace with them." She watches Dr. Mandel's reaction. Was this what the doctor wanted her to feel?

"In that case, there's one important thing you still have to do," says Dr. Mandel.

"And then I can go home?"

"No, after you go home."

Dani lets go of the swing. She smiles at Dr. Mandel. "What is that?" she asks.

Dr. Mandel watches a small boy shimmy up the leg of the swing set, fall, and try again.

"You must be at peace with Alex."

part 6 HOME

129

Partway through Dani's intensive therapy, she returned to the hotel to find Beth sobbing facedown on the couch.

"What's wrong, Mom?" she asked.

"Dr. Mandel called," Beth said.

"And?"

"She told me to stop locking my door at night. She said it wasn't helping you, even if you asked me to do it. She said it was the wrong thing to do."

"And that makes you sad?" Dani asked.

"No," her mother said. "It makes me happy."

"That's good," said Dani, sitting beside her. "I don't think I've made you happy in a while. I was starting to wonder if you wished you'd had two kids instead of one."

Beth patted Dani's knee. "She explained more of her technique. I think I understand her approach now. I guess she knows what she's doing."

Now they're packing to go home. They wander in and out of each other's rooms, returning what they borrowed.

For Dani, getting to know Boston has been the upside of these three weeks. The downsides have been missing Gordy and dreading what life will be like when she gets back. Dani is sure Gordy will be happy to see her. Nathan too. As far as everybody else, she knows only what she's been able to glean on the Internet. Tomorrow will be Dani's last session, and Beth will accompany her. For the rest of the summer Dani will see Dr. Mandel once a week, taking the train from Hawthorne. She likes the idea of coming back to her favorite parks and her favorite bakery and her favorite take-out place. She feels like she belongs here now.

130

Beth holds Dani's hand in Dr. Mandel's office. Holding your mother's hand at this age is silly but comforting at the same time. Dani supposes her mother is nervous.

"There's going to be homework," Dr. Mandel begins. "The key to Dani's recovery will be that she continue to practice what we've been doing once she gets home. If she stops working on the treatment, she will begin backsliding. If she stops trying altogether, she may end up where she was."

"I feel like I'm getting better," Dani says. "I want to continue."

"What does she have to do?" her mother asks.

"Dani needs to keep exposing herself to the people and situations that make her anxious and provoke her intrusive thoughts. She has to stay in those situations regardless of whether she has the thoughts. And she must resist performing any compulsions, such as hiding knives, locking the door between herself and another person, checking someone she may have harmed, feeling her mouth, or squeezing her hands. Eventually, with enough exposure, her anxiety will subside. Her thoughts will wax and wane, but Dani has the tools to keep them from overwhelming her."

"That sounds manageable," Beth says, clutching Dani's hand like it's something precious. "I wish the thoughts would go away completely, but I'm glad for any improvement. You've been wonderful."

Dr. Mandel cleans her glasses. "I'm going to work with you today, Beth, on helping Dani practice at home."

Beth smiles. She gets out her phone to take notes.

"The first thing you have to do is to arrange for Dani to see Alex."

"Alex?" Beth looks up from her phone.

Dr. Mandel waits.

"I don't think we can do that," Beth says. "I don't think we would want to."

Dr. Mandel clasps her hands over her knee. "Beth, Dani can handle it. She has already spent time with other children as practice. Now it must be Alex specifically. Alex is the person who arouses the most anxiety in Dani, so Alex is the person she has to be around."

Beth looks crestfallen. "But I don't see how that can work. If seeing Alex is a problem, why doesn't she just avoid him? It wouldn't be that difficult. I would even move to another town to reduce the chances of seeing him, if Dani would be less anxious. The only reason I'm not pursuing that is that Dani will be starting college in a year. We have only a year to get through."

"I know it's weird, Mom," Dani says. "In fact, the idea of it is making me really anxious. But Dr. Mandel has put me in some tough situations. This is just one more." Dani didn't tell Beth that in the final session Dr. Mandel had her hold the big knife and imagine killing Alex. She felt a twinge of worry that Beth wouldn't understand.

"What kind of anxiety is this bringing up for you, Dani?" Dr. Mandel asks.

"I'm afraid that when I see Alex I'll have thoughts of killing him again." She starts to squeeze her hands, then stops herself.

"Still?" Beth shuts her phone and drops her head in her hands.

"That's to be expected," Dr. Mandel says.

"Well, how would we arrange this?" Beth asks. "Would I call Alex's mother and say, 'My daughter wants to sit around and contemplate murdering your son'?"

"I feel terrible, Mom. I'm sorry." Dani starts to wonder if there's some way she can stay in Boston and not go home.

"No," Dr. Mandel says. "You arrange for a supervised visit between Dani and Alex, with both you and Alex's mom present. It would be best if this could be several visits. And Alex's mother should be told what the issues are and what the treatment plan is, so she can buy into it. You can invite her to see me for an explanation, if you and Dani are comfortable with that."

"I can't believe what you're asking me to do," Beth says. "This is going to be the hardest conversation I've ever had."

"If you like, you can avoid having that conversation by having his mom call me and I will explain it to her. You have some choices as to how to bring her on board. Another option would be to have the supervised visit here in my office. The five of us would meet together."

"But either way," Beth says, "you're saying I have to tell Alex's mother that Dani needs to see Alex. You know, in addition to this being uncomfortable for me, there's a good chance that she'll flat-out say no."

"You can do it, Mom," Dani says. "You're a professional salesperson. You can talk anyone into anything." But inside she is cringing too. She still feels ashamed. She doesn't want to face Mrs. Alex again. She would like it better if Dr. Mandel were with them to run interference.

"Well, I'll try," Beth says. "I'll try and I'll let you know."

They spend the rest of the session discussing the home practices Dani will do without Alex. Then it's time to go. Dani takes one final look at the view of Commonwealth Avenue. She feels like her world has gotten bigger here.

131

Beth is fixated on returning to town in the North Shore Landscaping truck. She tells Dani she's pleased that leaving her own car at the house made people believe she and Dani were farther away than they were. Sean double-parks at the hotel and comes to find them in the lobby. At first he walks right past Dani.

"Sorry," he says. "I forgot about the hair." He takes their bags and waits with Dani in the truck while Beth goes to return the rental car she's used while in Boston.

"Are you feeling better?" Sean asks. He looks her up and down for proof that she's changed.

Sean's question sounds awkward. Most likely Beth encouraged him to ask it. Beth has always wanted Dani and Sean in a semi-stepfather/stepdaughter relationship befitting the friendship ring. But Beth doesn't know that her pushing Sean only makes him dislike Dani more.

Dani realizes that she has rarely had thoughts of killing Sean. The perversity of her illness caused her to have thoughts of harming mostly people she liked or loved.

"What's going on back home?" she says, maintaining a neutral expression.

"No more TV trucks in town, thank God," Sean says. "No

more reporters following me and anyone else who knows you around the supermarket or the gas station. I actually went to a movie last night. But I wish your mother had joined me. I'm looking forward to having her back again."

"What did you see?" Dani forces herself to ask.

"Some animated thing," he mutters. Clearly this was not the question he had wanted her to ask.

Sean makes a noise in his throat. "You know," he begins again, "I've been thinking of asking your mother to marry me."

"You've been considering that for a while, haven't you?" Dani asks.

"Actually we put an engagement on the back burner because she's been so occupied with you."

Dani hears the unspoken phrase "and your problems." It bugs her that Sean seems to be using her as an excuse. "You should be thanking me instead," she says.

Sean is startled. He looks up the street to see if Beth is coming.

"You could thank me for making it possible for you to delay marrying my mom. If she knew how long this was going to take, she might have looked around for someone else."

"We'll at least wait until you're off to college," Sean says. He grimaces and wiggles his head like he's withholding the rest: *if you don't screw it all up between now and then.*

Dani doesn't take the bait.

"Anyway," Sean continues, "Beth says you're coming back to Boston once a week. Please don't talk her into buying you any more clothes or anything. She's spending a bundle on the lawyer as it is."

"Well, you know what? The lawyer is just a technicality." Dani rolls down her window. "I haven't done anything wrong."

"Not yet."

"Not yet? What's that supposed to mean?" Dani knows exactly what it means, but she doesn't argue. She realizes that just as Sean should thank her for helping him remain single, she should thank Sean for offending her. It makes her realize that even though her mind doesn't work perfectly, she's still entitled to basic human decency.

"Beth would kill me for saying that," Sean mutters, watching the traffic. "You know, I can't imagine what it's like to have . . . to go through something like what you're going through. It must be tough to even get up in the morning if your brain is all messed up."

Dani tries to accept that this is Sean's attempt at an apology, but she can't resist comparing him to her dad, who made her feel like she was the coolest, cleverest, and most athletic daughter in the universe . . . right up until the day he left. At first she didn't realize what would change when her father divorced her mom. Then she found out it meant that he was divorcing both of them.

"Listen, Sean," Dani says. "I need you to do something. My treatment isn't over yet, and my mom and I still have rough times ahead. We need people we can really rely on. So think about whether you can be that person. If you're going to be into my mother, be really into her."

Beth is at the hotel door.

"Here we are, darling," Sean calls.

132

Shelley and Meghan return to practice at the handball court. Meghan has no aptitude for tennis, but she's determined to give it another shot. Say what you will about Meghan, she believes in herself and she keeps bouncing back. She's what Mr. Gabler calls "a trouper."

"Sam called me last night," Meghan announces.

"Sam?"

"My ex-boyfriend, the singer-songwriter. He wants to see me over the summer."

"Is he coming up here?" Shelley asks. "Maybe a bunch of us can go to a concert or something."

"No, we talked about my going back to Pennsylvania for a while. I called a couple of my girlfriends too. I'll probably go back to visit for six weeks."

Six weeks? Shelley has a dropping feeling, like her feet and knees are turning numb. "Are you getting back together with him? I guess the prospect of somebody writing songs for you must be pretty appealing."

"Not getting back together, per se," Meghan says, hitting her return over the wall. "But we want to see whether there's anything there."

Shelley runs after Meghan's stray ball so that Meghan won't

see her expression. In the past few days she's come to accept that Meghan won't be her first real girlfriend. But she had looked forward to hanging out with her all summer anyway. Now that won't happen either.

You have to be a trouper, Shelley tells herself. *You have to bounce back too. Look at you this last month, having to be your own best friend. Look at everything you've done. This is the closest you've come to having someone of your own. I think that's brave. You're getting somewhere. You're making progress. A year from now you'll be starting college. It will be easier then.*

133

Dani goes for a run, trading her coastal roads for an inland route where no one will expect her. It would be better to run in a pack, but she doesn't have a pack to run in.

As she starts to feel a pleasant burn in her calves and quads, she turns onto a street with no houses, mostly small industries like a gravel company, a tool-and-die place, and auto-repair shops. She remembers how great it had been to run along the Charles, feeling like part of a huge exercising body with the river as its artery. In English class Ms. Martin once assigned the memoir of a gay man who moved from a small farming town to the East Village in New York City. Dani had loved that book. Her three weeks in Boston made her understand how people can lose themselves in the anonymity of a city. It must be one of the best ways of starting over.

A car pulls beside Dani and honks. Dani looks for a side street to escape down. She's ready for something to be yelled at her or thrown at her.

"It's all right," the driver says. "I'm a supporter."

"Oh!" She never expected that. "Thank you." She wipes her face with the back of her arm.

"You're Dani. The girl in the newspapers."

"That's right."

"You changed your hair."

He's a youngish guy in a suit, a business guy. He has a nice car, an Audi.

"Do you have a minute?" he asks.

"I guess," she says.

"Because I think you and I are two of a kind."

"What do you mean?" Dani asks, leaning in the window and moving her feet to keep her heart rate up.

He begins a story about when he was in junior high, a horrendous story involving a neighbor's pet cat and some power tools. At first Dani doesn't get what he's saying, because of the pleasant look on his face. "You're my kind of person," he says.

"I'm not your kind of person," she says, moving away.

"I have a couple more stories like that," he continues. "Would you like to hear them?"

"Let me go," Dani says, even though the driver hasn't confined her in any way. The nearest side street has a dead end. She sprints across the yard of a business selling concrete fountains and benches, steps on a bench to vault over the chain-link fence, and runs out of sight of the driver. But she can't run away from the thought that he recognized something in her. That even despite Dr. Mandel's help, deep inside she *is* like him; they *could* be two of a kind. It's a relief to meet someone whose thoughts are uglier than hers.

134

When Dani gets home Sean isn't there. She and her mother have baked fish and a big salad for dinner. Dani doesn't tell Beth what happened on her run. It would only make Beth worry, and Dani would be under house arrest again. She'll get Gordy to run with her next time.

"We need to talk about senior year," Beth says. "If you want, you can finish high school somewhere else. Do you want to try a private school? It's late in the game, but we may be able to call in a few favors."

Dani pours blue cheese dressing over her salad. Unlike her mother, she has never been on a diet.

"I don't know," she replies. "I guess I'm hoping to finish here. My friends are here, after all. And you. You're here."

"You could go to school in the city if you want," Beth answers. "You could even live there. We'll see."

Dani takes a slice of warm bread from the basket on the table.

"We have a meeting with the lawyer tomorrow at four," Beth tells her.

"What do you think he'll say?"

"That we have a shot at a lawsuit. Against the newspaper if not the police department."

Dani skates a piece of lettuce in the pool of dressing on her plate. "I thought we were seeing Alex tomorrow. Mom, have you even made plans with Mrs. Alex yet?"

"No." Beth crinkles her face as if this is something she forgot.

"You have to, Mom. I need to see Alex so I can get better."

"I know, Dani. I just . . . I don't know what to say. What do you say in a situation like this? Actually, I'm wondering if the lawyer will tell us that's a bad idea. Can't Dr. Mandel come up with a different form of treatment?"

"You have to call Mrs. Alex, Mom. Or get Dr. Mandel to do it. She says we have to keep moving forward."

"I know, I know. I'll call her tomorrow morning. We'll see her first, even if only for fifteen minutes, before we go to the lawyer. A quick hello to get the ball rolling. I'll try to set something up for three o'clock."

"You're really going to call?"

"I am. It's as good as done."

Dani feels anxious when she goes to bed. She's missed Alex, but she dreads the thoughts she'll have when she's in the same room with him. *Be strong*, she tells herself. *The only way out is through.*

135

"Have you called Mrs. Alex?" Dani asks her mom at breakfast the next morning. "Are we meeting her at three?"

"I'll call her as soon as I get to the office," Beth says. She grabs her phone and keys and heads to her morning appointments.

136

"You don't want to run along the water?" Gordy says after he hugs Dani for a long time.

"I don't want to be recognized," Dani says.

"I like your hair like that, by the way. You look sort of French." They start on a different inland route, past the town green and the colonial cemetery.

"You know," Gordy continues, "nobody's going to bother you if you're with me. I won't let anyone hurt you."

Dani smiles. Gordy wants to protect her. But what does he really know about people wanting to hurt one another? She doesn't tell him about the Audi guy because he would be too upset.

She remembers reading about women who have been raped and how they never wanted to have sex with their husbands again. Some husbands didn't understand, and they ended up divorcing their wives and finding someone else. After what she's been through, she and Gordy might be like those people. What can they do to keep from drifting apart?

Her thoughts wander to later this afternoon and what it will be like seeing Alex after all this time. She's nervous about seeing him, but she's afraid to see Mrs. Alex. Of all the people in town, she dreads Mrs. Alex the most.

137

Beth Solomon looks at her phone. It's one o'clock already and she still hasn't made the call. She didn't lie to Dani about calling; she fully intended to see Alex and Mrs. Alex. However, she just can't bring herself to call Mrs. Alex. She has called plenty of people in her life. She's made many calls that took a lot of guts. She's given people bad news of all kinds, in business and otherwise. But this has to be the hardest call she's ever been required to make.

The fact is that she's ashamed to call Mrs. Alex. When Dr. Mandel suggested it she cringed, and ever since they left Boston the necessity of the call has hung over her head like a punishment. Every aspect of this phone call makes her run from it. As a mother, she has to call another mother whose child has been threatened. She has to suggest that this mother put her child in jeopardy again. And even if Dani is no danger to anyone, her problems all must point to Beth in some way. She has not seen or spoken to Cynthia since the incident, and she knows what Cynthia must think of her. But Beth has never had to find out in person. Maybe Dani is getting better, and will continue to get better. But the bottom line is that Beth feels utterly ashamed, and she is unable to look Mrs. Alex in the eye.

She needs to call Dani, and Dr. Mandel if necessary, and ask for more time.

138

Dani and Gordy stop in a weird little mom-and-pop store for an ice cream soda.

"Geez," Dani says, "this is like the store that time forgot. Who comes in here?"

"Just people looking for cigarettes and porn," Gordy says. "I'm sorry, that was crude."

They sit at the counter on two sticky stools. "It isn't Icey's," Gordy says, "but it is ice cream."

"I've never had bad ice cream, have you?" Dani asks.

"There's no such thing," Gordy agrees. "You'll be back at Icey's soon. You'll be back everywhere soon, when people realize you're still the kind, beautiful, sensitive, awesome girl they always thought you were. And I'm going to buy you the biggest ice cream at Icey's to celebrate."

"The Kitchen Sink Sundae?"

"Yep. It's got like twenty-eight scoops of ice cream in it."

"And it costs about fifty bucks."

"So what? We'll each have one." He gives her a cold peck on the cheek. "I'm just glad to have you back."

Dani grabs his arm and looks at his watch. "My God, it's two thirty already. I've gotta go. I've got an appointment."

"Not with your other boyfriend, I hope?"

Gordy's playfulness is annoying. He has no idea about the kind of attention she's gotten from men since the newspaper article. Not just that Audi driver. Lately her MyFace account has received numerous love letters, two nude male photos, and one marriage proposal. One person even wrote to her mom to see if an introduction could be arranged. It was hideous, absolutely hideous, the kind of people who thought they deserved her.

"Run again tomorrow?" Dani asks Gordy. "In the morning. Let's try somewhere out of town."

She jogs toward Alex's. It will be great to see him and to know that she doesn't have to worry anymore. It will be like starting over. But it will be weird and uncomfortable too. She hopes making the phone call wasn't too awful for Mom.

139

Beth has been trying to call Dani. She stops at the house and sees that Dani left her phone at home.

140

Alex is the first to answer the door.

"It's her, Mom!" he yells. He pumps his fist. *"Ye-es!*

"You didn't move away?" he asks Dani. "Or did you move away and then move here?"

"I was away temporarily," Dani says. "For a few weeks." She'd love to hug Alex, but she stays several feet away on the front step.

Mrs. Alex comes to the door with her busy face on.

"I'm sorry I'm all sweaty," Dani says.

At first Mrs. Alex doesn't recognize Dani. Then it's as if a metal security gate clamps down from the ceiling. She swoops Alex onto her shoulder.

"Put me down! Put me down! I can't see!" Alex kicks his feet and twists around to face Dani. Mrs. Alex slides him onto the floor behind her and partly closes the door.

"How is your treatment going?" Mrs. Alex asks.

"Pretty well. My mom should be here in a few minutes."

Mrs. Alex looks confused. "Your mom?"

"Didn't she call you?"

Mrs. Alex stands up straight, like she's made of armor. "No. You mean recently? *No*."

Dani spins around on her heel. "Shoot!" she says. "Oh, *Mom*."

She feels like cursing Beth out, not in an OCD way but in a regular teenage way, for putting her in this position. "She was supposed to call you about, you know, what happened, and figuring everything out . . ." Dani realizes she should be using better language for this. She should be using the words Dr. Mandel used. "Oh God, I don't even have my phone!"

"You changed your hair," Mrs. Alex observes.

"I had to."

"I hate April," Alex says, from behind the door. "She hogs the computer."

"That's too bad," Dani says. "I should go."

"No, wait," Mrs. Alex says. "Do you want me to call Beth? I'll see if she wants to get together like you expected. It'll just take a minute."

"That would be great," Dani says. "If this is an okay time." She can't believe Mrs. Alex is being so helpful. Dani feels the way Layla Amundsen must have felt. She's being more open with people and they're helping. They're listening.

"Come on in," Mrs. Alex says. "Why don't you wait in Alex's room?"

Mrs. Alex seems uncomfortable with the idea of Dani and Beth being here, but Dani expected that. Like Beth said, it's going to be awkward at first. But they all need to get re-exposed to one another. Then, just like in Dr. Mandel's office, the anxiety level will start going down. Cynthia steps outside, clutching Alex.

"Let me go," Alex says. "I want to go upstairs with Dani."

Dani walks through the messy living room, up the familiar carpeted stairs, and into Alex's room. His bed with the Spider-Man sheets is unmade, so she straightens the sheets and comforter. Too bad about April. Dani had never been a computer hog. She had allowed Alex to do pretty much whatever he wanted. The therapist here in Hawthorne, Dr. Kumar, had tried to suggest that Dani had allowed Alex to walk all over her and that had made her angry. But even now she isn't sure she would do it differently. So she's a pushover when it comes to little kids. How can you fight your own nature?

Dani slips off her sneakers and rubs her feet, the same way Mrs. Alex used to. The sandals she wore in the city looked great but they did a job on her skin. She hears a car pull up in front of the house and another one leave. Is Beth here already? The sound of someone digging in a drawer downstairs. Was Mrs. Alex missing her keys again? The front door opens and closes, and she hears steps on the carpeted stairs. The bedroom door opens, and someone steps inside. It's Malcolm Pinto, but Dani barely recognizes him. In a tidy blue shirt and pants, he looks like a cross between a mall security guard and an evangelist.

"Hey, Malcolm. What are you doing here?" Dani asks, still rubbing her feet.

"Hey, Dani." Malcolm closes the door behind him. He's carrying a backpack made of camouflage material.

"Are you babysitting now?" Dani asks him. "I thought they hired someone named April."

"No, I'm not babysitting. I'm not the babysitter. You're the

Babysitter." He's looking at her so intently that it confirms what she has sometimes suspected, that he has a crush on her. The prospect is not very appealing.

"Who let you in?" Dani asks. "Mrs. Draper and I were going to have a talk with my mom."

"Mrs. Draper drove away. Didn't you hear the car?"

"Well, why are you here? You're making me uncomfortable." She tugs her sneakers back on, contemplates making some flimsy excuse and going back downstairs. Maybe she'll wait for Beth in the living room.

"It's about to get a lot more uncomfortable," Malcolm says. He hovers in his usual way, like a string bean on a vine, with his pack over one shoulder and his hands in his back pockets. She wonders if he might be stoned. He smiles with that annoying look he has on the quad, as if he can sort all the girls into this type and that type. She wonders if he's rocking the usual tobacco fleck between his teeth.

"What are you talking about?" Dani stands up, allowing the irritation to show in her voice.

"This is what I'm talking about." He takes a piece of paper from his pack. It reads:

PROTECT OUR KIDS

"Hold it up," he says.

"You're involved with POK?" Dani asks. "Oh, for Christ's sake, Malcolm."

He digs into his pack for a piece of tape and sticks the paper to her T-shirt.

"Hey, keep away from me." She tears off the sign, but he's taking her picture with his phone.

"Are you going to sell that to someone?" Dani asks, trying to grab the phone out of his hands. "Is that what you want? All the lowlifes are coming out of the woodwork. Get out of my way."

"Not this time, Dani," Malcolm says. He pockets the phone and pulls a pair of handcuffs from his bag. "My dad wasn't allowed to do the job. But somebody has to."

He tries to grab her wrists, but Dani's too fast for him. He laughs, shakes his head like an indulgent parent, and pulls something else from his pack—a black handle with a glinting blade. Could it be Cynthia's kitchen knife, *the* knife? Was that the clatter Dani heard downstairs?

"Looks familiar, doesn't it?" Malcolm says. "Now are you ready to cooperate?"

"Wait, Malcolm," Dani whispers.

"What?"

"Please make sure Alex won't hear."

"He's gone. He left with Mrs. Draper. I saw them."

"Are you sure? I'm not so sure. Maybe Mrs. Draper left by herself. Please make sure he isn't anywhere in the house. You wouldn't want him to hear. He's just a little kid, Malcolm."

Malcolm looks confused. He glances at the bedroom door, and in that moment Dani lunges at the floor and grabs the junior racket she bought for Alex. Gripping it with her two-fisted backhand, she whacks the edge into the side of Malcolm's neck, aiming for an artery.

"Where—," he says, and slumps on the bed.

Dani spreads her feet, improving her stance.

"I'm sorry, Malcolm," she says, and whacks him again, this time on the back of the head.

Later, when the police arrive, after Dani calls them herself to tell them she hit Malcolm, when Michael Pinto walks into the room and yells "Malky!" and Dani apologizes to him and Malcolm over and over again, Dani will feel grateful that Mrs. Alex wasn't too neat around the house. Because if she had been in the habit of putting things away, the tennis racket may not have been exactly where Dani left it, and Dani would be in much worse trouble now.

epilogue

141

Tuesday, June 15

Hawthorne *Beacon-Times*

Opinion

By Shelley Dietrich

WHO CAN YOU TELL YOUR SECRETS TO?

A friend once wanted to tell me a secret. The friend was Dani Solomon, and although I didn't realize it, she was asking me for help. She had a problem with her mind. That was her secret, and that was what she needed to tell me. The problem wasn't obvious, and no one else knew. She was trusting me with something delicate, a delicate situation.

I was busy and preoccupied. I didn't see what she was trying to tell me, and when I did pay attention I turned it into something else. I didn't realize that the essence of who my friend was would never change. I didn't realize how much I would miss her, even with that problem.

What is bothering me today is that I didn't listen to Dani, and I didn't respect Dani's secret. When people started talking about Dani, I did too. We get so much training in school about watching out for people who might be dangerous. I told myself that, by believing what people said and discussing Dani's secret, I was protecting others.

I also told Dani a secret. I'm pretty sure she kept my secret. It was a big one, but possibly not as painful as what she had to carry.

If there is anyone who can be trusted with your secrets, it would have to be your best friend. Now, partly because of what I did and didn't do, I'm starting the summer without my best friend. This year Dani and I will not be going to the beach, driving my mother's car along the back shore singing at the top of our lungs, or reading magazines with our feet stuck in my brother Ralphie's pool.

Who can you tell your secrets to, Dani? Try your best friend. Try giving me another chance.

Shelley Dietrich is a junior at Hawthorne High School.

142

Wednesday, June 16

National Envestigator News

BACK TO SCHOOL FOR SICKO SITTER

Disturbed Teen Returns as Cops Grumble

143

Dani and Shelley sit in the courtyard with their dips. It's the last week of classes, and Dani wants to prepare for finals. Media trucks line the main road near school but they can't come onto school property. Dani found the words *Baby Killer* on her locker. A few people yelled "Sicko!" "Whack job!" and "Headcase!" One imitated a child screaming. All morning kids have taken photos and videos of her and sent them God knows where. Two kids yelled "Way to go!" and gave her the thumbs-up as she walked by. Dani doesn't know if that means they like dark hair or if they believe in child-killing or if they enjoyed the entertainment of the past few weeks.

But no one can touch Dani, because Shelley is acting as her bodyguard, walking Dani to all her classes. In music group both Gordon and Nathan hovered protectively until they saw Shelley had it covered. Mr. Gabler shook her hand and didn't can her for missing the last concert. Meghan screamed and hugged Dani, as if Dani was a childhood friend from Pennsylvania.

144

Malcolm Pinto, his head and neck bandaged, observes Dani and Shelley from the edge of the school property, near the TV trucks. The summer doesn't look promising. Because he's suspended from school, he will have to take summer classes with young violators his father calls "hardened." He's been charged with assault with a dangerous weapon and has to stay five hundred yards away from Dani for the next six months, which will mean missing all the best concerts and the Fourth of July bonfire. His father is trying to get the charges reduced, while Dani's lawyer is suing both the PD and the newspaper for revealing too much information. Michael Pinto wants to persuade the local media that Malcolm was well-meaning but misguided, caught up in a frenzy that gripped the entire town. That he made some mistakes but he genuinely believed he was protecting someone. Malcolm believes that, in private, his father has to be a little bit proud of him.

Malcolm's father has some choice words for Dani and her rich mother, even her father out in Colorado. At the very least, this incident will damage Malcolm's chances of getting into the police academy. But Malcolm has no regrets. Throwing a rock through a window, even holding a knife to someone, is nothing compared to the murder of a little kid. And murders are prevented every day by ordinary people who carry no badge. Maybe with the connections Malcolm has now, the opportunities will come knocking.

145

"So," Dani says, dipping corn chips into cream cheese, "did you tell Meghan or anyone else what I said about Mr. Gabler?"

"No." Shelley's been staring up at the third-floor windows, but she looks straight at Dani. "I said I wouldn't tell, and I didn't."

"Thanks," Dani says. She offers Shelley some banana slices with honey. "So what ended up happening between the two of you?"

"My feelings got really intense. But it turned out she had a boyfriend back where she used to live." She waits to be drawn out.

"In Pennsylvania?" Dani asks.

"That's right, Hartswell, Pennsylvania. So any time she was with me she would be texting him on the side. And now she's going back to Hartswell for the summer. She's going to spend it with her boyfriend. But she keeps saying she's going to miss me."

Shelley looks at the third floor again and pauses. Dani isn't sure what to say.

"She ended up being a big disappointment," Shelley continues. "But it was kind of great for a while. I can't even tell you. I've never felt so alive."

"And I missed it all," Dani says, dipping a banana slice in honey for Shelley.

"Toward the end I was on the verge of telling her about me, but now I'm glad I didn't. You're still the only person I ever told. Did you tell anyone about me, after that day?" Shelley asks, looking serious, almost frightened.

Now it's Dani's turn to avoid eye contact. She takes a deep breath.

"I sort of did," she says.

Shelley pulls up straight. She has a milder version of the air-gun look. "You told somebody I was gay? Why?"

"I had to tell my doctors so I could get better."

"What does my being gay have to do with you getting better?"

Dani can never tell Shelley about her urge to yell *dyke* and *lesbo*. That would be too hurtful. "It's kind of complicated," she says. "But my doctors aren't allowed to tell anyone, so trust me, no rumors will be coming back to you. Look, I'm really sorry. Can we say we're even and move on from here?"

"Deal," Shelley says.

Dani thinks about the thousand chances a person has each day to cross lines, and how people draw those lines in different places. Shelley is back in Dani's circle now, and Alex and Mrs. Alex are out. But no one has only one circle. Each person has several overlapping circles like the Olympic rings, with some important others in circles off to the side that you barely see. Dani will always be in a side circle of Mrs. Alex's, because Mrs. Alex will always keep her eye on Dani. Alex will always be in Dani's side circle because she will always care about him. In the days since she crowned Malcolm, Dani's been aware of Alex's sneakers flashing in the periphery of her sight, pulled into a car or tugged around a supermarket aisle. The flash of his sneakers is like the smile of the Cheshire Cat in *Alice in Wonderland*. It doesn't fade away, and Dani feels that the universe is winking at her.

AUTHOR'S NOTE

I wrote this book because, like Dani Solomon, I left a babysitting job because I had unwanted and persistent thoughts about harming the children. Also like Dani, I had trouble finding a therapist who recognized my symptoms. One counselor I phoned was afraid to meet me, and another asked whether I heard voices in my television set telling me to kill people (he thought I was psychotic).

Fortunately, I found a therapist who used a variety of techniques to help me in all areas of my life over a two-year period. We discussed some form of obsessive-compulsive disorder (OCD) as a possible reason for my symptoms, but we considered other causes as well. Not until ten years later, when my librarian sister came across the book *The Imp of the Mind: Exploring the Silent Epidemic of Obsessive Bad Thoughts* by Lee Baer Ph.D. (Dutton, 2001), did I see my symptoms framed definitively as OCD.

Ten more years have gone by, and the bad-thoughts form of OCD is still not on the map of people's awareness. Why? Because the public, and even most doctors and therapists, continue to understand OCD in terms of germ phobias, counting, and hand-washing. In fact, of the approximately eighty people to whom I told the book's premise ("It's about a babysitter who's tormented by thoughts of harming the child she cares for"), only one person asked, "Is it about OCD?" If I had said, "It's about a teenage girl who can't function because she's constantly washing her hands," nearly everyone I spoke to would have asked that question.

This book is intended as more than bibliotherapy. Dani's situation contains tensions and paradoxes that simply make for a great story. I had been able to go away and heal in private. But what if a teen girl's most horrifying secret thoughts became public . . . were talked about at school . . . were broadcast on the TV news and in national newspapers?

The dramatic treatment Dani undergoes in Boston with Dr. Mandel is real. It's called exposure and response prevention (ERP) therapy. Kimberly Glazier of Yeshiva University, a therapist and researcher who advised me on the technical aspects of the novel, told me that ERP is "the gold standard" for treating OCD. The best way to overcome this illness is by exposing oneself to the triggering situations rather than avoiding them, and that's what brings the story to what I hope is an exciting climax.

I hope too that teachers and readers will use this book to discuss whether thoughts are equivalent to deeds and whether people should be punished for their thoughts. Laws and religions attempt to answer this question, but perhaps teen readers can answer it even better.

Readers who want to know more about obsessive-compulsive disorder and its treatment should read Baer's book *Getting Control* (Plume, 2012) or visit the website of the International OCD Foundation (ocfoundation.org).

J. R. Y.

Can love be real if you've never met?

An exclusive look at Janet Ruth Young's next powerful novel.

she was

She was a girl talking to me in the dark.

Everybody knows what happened with my parents. Everybody I talk to when I call.

"You can turn your life around," I had told her. "Starting today, you can be free. You can do anything you want. Don't you see that?"

I'm down, but I'm not out. I'm a fighter. On my good days, few can defeat me.

"I admire that about you," I had told her.

I remember every compliment you ever gave me. Especially when you said I was strong.

"I have to go. Will you be okay?"

I'll handle it. I always do. Good night, sweet Hallmark prince.

new directions

Where is everyone?" Dad asked when he got home. It was October 25, and he had just come from his therapy appointment. Dad looked good these days, like someone who had a purpose. He shaved in the morning and dressed for work in a jacket and tie and Rockport loafers. He stood straighter and was no longer bony. His felty red hair was cut short, so that it verged on stylish, and he wore a sharp, arrowlike goatee. He worked as a draftsman at Liberty Fixtures, a company that made shelving for department stores. He looked a lot like me, if I were fifty and had accepted that I would always hate the job I needed.

I was just in from a bike ride. Mom and Linda were making pizza and salad for supper. Dad dropped a bag marked ART SUPPLIES on the dining room table. You could hear the rush-hour traffic going by out back; the highway ran right behind our house.

Drive past our house: the bright orange door, the brass

knocker in the shape of a salamander (unnecessary because we have a functioning doorbell), our name and house number (Morrison 32) painted in black Gothic lettering on a white rock at the end of the driveway—that's all Linda's work. And Mom directed a museum. We might as well have a sign outside saying Artistic People Live Here. Right now Linda and Mom were laying the pepperoni slices in overlapping circles to look like a chrysanthemum. The art supplies could have been for almost anyone—anyone but me.

"I'm going to paint again," Dad said. He looked quietly fierce, like a gladiator before the lion is let out.

"Yippee!" Linda danced around, wriggling and elfish. She switched from teenager mode to little girl mode when she wanted to feel closer to my parents.

Mom dried her hands and wrapped her arms around Dad's middle.

"That's exciting, honey. But you've always painted."

"I mean get *serious* about painting. I want to be in the art world again. I put my art aside. Because of the needs of making a living and raising a family."

Excuse me for being born, I thought.

"That's a sad story," Linda said. Linda's style reworked droopy clothes that had belonged to an elderly person, which made her look younger than thirteen. She came up to Dad's armpit, and she had a wormy way of sharing his space. Now she slipped her hand into Dad's, and he held it in the air like it was a prize. I was as tall as he was, so he never looked at me, or my hand, that way.

"I never stopped you," Mom said. "I never told you you couldn't paint." Like Linda, Mom worked to separate herself from the run of humanity. She wore her black hair perfectly straight, wore dark lipstick, and owned only necklaces that were one of a kind. Usually they were made for her by someone noteworthy, such as a blind sculptor, a poetry-writing shepherd, or a male nun.

"Of course not, sweetie," Dad said. He crinkled his eyes at Mom, like he was winking to make her admit a lie.

"Don't forget, Bill, I fell in love with you over *Inverted Horizon*."

"I'm not forgetting."

Inverted Horizon was the ocean-on-top sunset painting of Dad's that was shown by a Fifty-Seventh Street gallery in New York City when Mom was in graduate school and Dad was working at a paint store. He ended up selling that to a collector, as well as his vertical sunset painting *Perpendicular Horizon*. He once told me that they were the best things he had ever done—part technical exercise, part making fun of the sunset cliché, and part, he said, "Just something great to look at."

At the opening reception, Mom stood in front of *Inverted Horizon* for a long time. A tall guy in an army fatigue jacket and tuxedo pants came along and stood beside her, and without his saying anything, she knew he was the painter. Although I don't like to view either of my parents as a love object, I always felt that was a good way to meet someone: nothing flashy or obvious, just a meeting of the minds and a sense of being immediately understood.

"Well, for the record," Mom continued, "I completely support your painting. As of today, as of right now, and for the future. Completely."

“I completely do too, Dad.” Linda scurried away from Dad and emptied the bag: tubes of paint, brushes, brush cleaner.

“Why all of a sudden?” I asked, leaning on one end of the table. I didn’t touch Dad or his art supplies. I knew enough to see that he had about three hundred dollars’ worth.

“Dr. Fritz and I talked about it. Art is my missing piece.” Dad pointed to the paints, then tapped a spot somewhere between his heart and his gut. “The missing piece of my emotional puzzle.”

“Are you sure this is a good idea?” I finally said.

“Why not?” he asked. A distinctive painting of a chicken, done by someone at Mom’s museum, hung on one wall. Anytime people came for dinner, they commented on the chicken. Dad’s gaze drifted to it, then back to me. A year ago he fit into my clothes. Now he had put weight on, even had a little belly forming.

“I would hate to see you get all excited and set yourself up . . .”

“Set myself up?” Dad pressed. Was he challenging me to say it?

“He’s fine now, Billy,” Mom said.

Dad spoke at the same time. “I painted thirty years ago.”

“I don’t want you to get too involved in it and then get upset. That’s all.”

“What would upset me? And even so, why can’t I get upset?”

Mom and Linda wouldn’t say it. But I didn’t want a repeat of last winter.

last winter: a memory

I've brought a new friend home after school. It's only two thirty, and I see Dad's car in the driveway. He must have come home early. I walk into the living room with my friend, expecting to introduce him to Dad. Gordon is so superb that I really want to impress him. He's new in town, and though some of the other new kids are snobby, Gordon isn't. He plays French horn and has played on the White House lawn with the All-State band. He seems confident and relaxed in every situation, and his hair seems exactly the same length every time I see him.

I hear Dad moving at the other end of the house, and call his name. In the past he's always had a story or joke for my friends. Sometimes he's played an aria from his collection of opera CDs. But this time he doesn't come.

"Just a minute," I tell Gordon. Finally Dad walks into the hall, but he doesn't look at Gordon or me. He goes past us, toward the den, rubbing his hands and whistling tunelessly. Now he's coming back again.

"Dad, stop a minute. I want you to meet someone."

"Are you looking for something, Mr. Morrison?" Gordon asks. "Can I help you find it?"

Gordon watches Dad with that game smile: relaxed, confident. But I begin to realize that Dad's walking and his whistling are involuntary, that some kind of worry is driving Dad from one end of the house to the other.

After a few minutes Gordy also realizes something is very wrong, something I haven't told him because I didn't know and I wouldn't know how to explain it if I did. He walks back to the bus stop with his instrument case and his backpack, and that is the last time I bring a friend home.

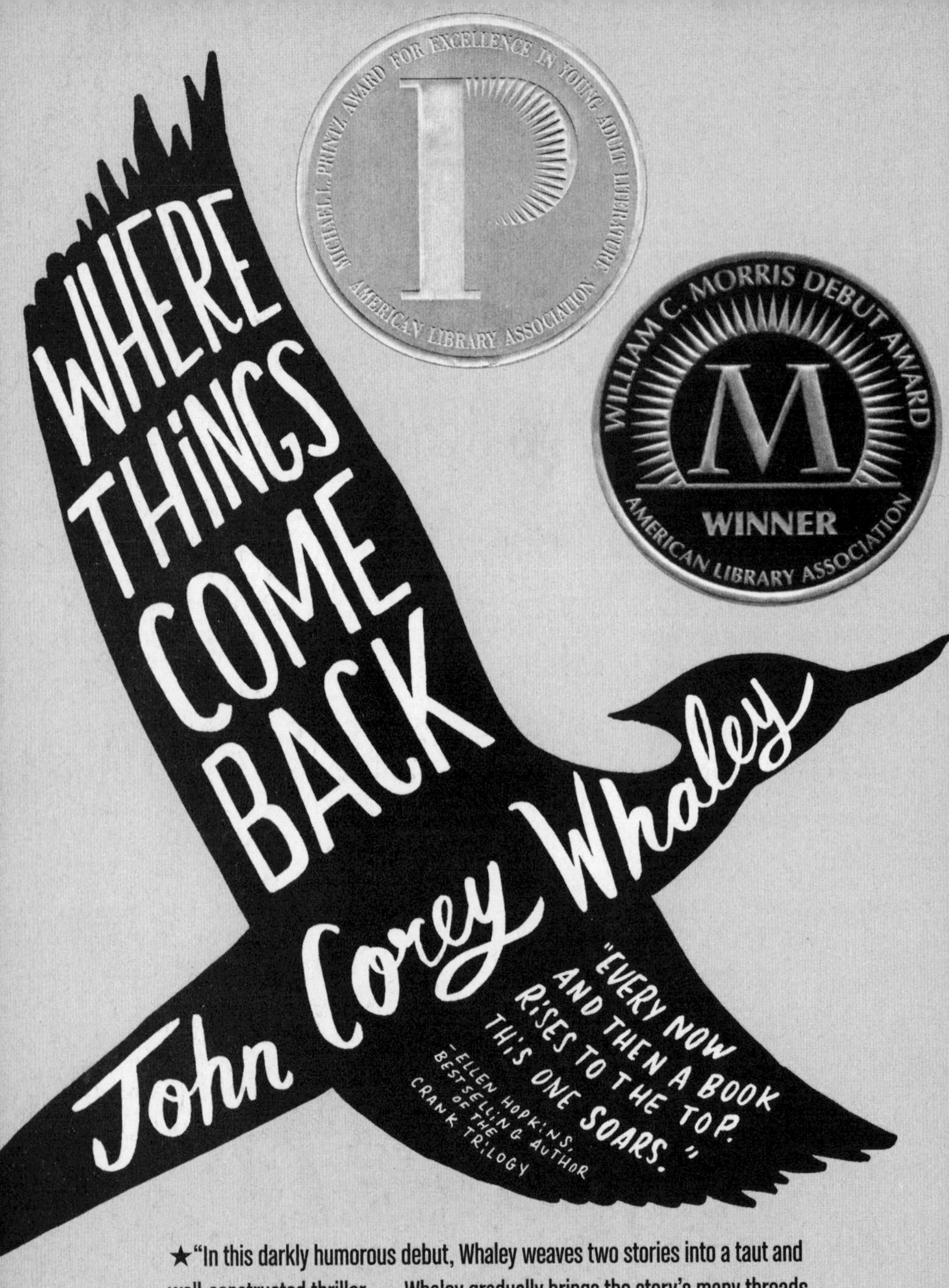

★"In this darkly humorous debut, Whaley weaves two stories into a taut and well-constructed thriller. . . . Whaley gradually brings the story's many threads together in a disturbing, heartbreaking finale that retains a touch of hope."
—**Publishers Weekly**, starred review

EBOOK EDITION ALSO AVAILABLE atheneum From Atheneum Books SimonandSchuster.com

Imagine you and your best friend head out west on a cross-country bike trek. Imagine that you get into a fight—and stop riding together. Imagine you reach Seattle, go back home, start college. Imagine you think your former best friend does too. Imagine he doesn't. Imagine your world shifting. . . .

★ "Fresh, absorbing, compelling."
—*Kirkus Reviews*, STARRED REVIEW

★ "Bradbury's keen details about the bike trip, the places, the weather, the food, the camping, and the locals add wonderful texture to this exciting first novel. . . ."
—*Booklist*, STARRED REVIEW

"The story moves quickly and will easily draw in readers."
—*School Library Journal*

"This is an intriguing summer mystery."—*Chicago Tribune*

"*Shift* is a wonderful book by a gifted author."
—teenreads.com

EBOOK EDITION ALSO AVAILABLE

Atheneum Books for Young Readers

TEEN.SimonandSchuster.com